AF166726

BISI
A UNIQUE AFRICAN GIRL
by
Jonathan Adedayo Odukoya
ISBN: 978-1-9163097-9-1

Copyright 2019
All rights reserved. No part of this publication may be reproduced, stored in a retrieval system or transmitted in any form or by any means, electronic, mechanical, photocopy, recording or otherwise, without prior written consent of the copyright owner. Nor can it be circulated in any form of binding or cover other than that in which it is published and without similar condition including this condition being imposed on a subsequent purchaser.
The right of Jonathan Adedayo Odukoya to be identified as the author of this work has been asserted in accordance with the Copyright Designs and Patents Act 1988.
A copy of this book is deposited with the British Library

Published By: -

i2i Publishing. Manchester.
www.i2ipublishing.co.uk

TABLE OF CONTENTS

CHAPTER 1: A CHILD IS BORN

The sun was shining at its peak. The wind was hardly blowing. The atmosphere was deadly still and hot. Plant leaves that were usually green and attractive during the rainy season were brownish due to the effect of the hot sun. A bird fluttered along a narrow footpath trying to catch a butterfly. The footpath led to Langbodo river, the only river serving Yawiri village. Yawiri was about one hundred and fifty kilometers from the populous city of Ibadan in Nigeria. It had a population of less than one thousand people and had only one primary school and a church. There was neither electricity nor pipe-borne water in the village. The nearest clinic was about one hundred kilometers away. Yawiri was a typical Yoruba village setting.

Abike emerged from the west end of the footpath that led to Langbodo river carrying a heavy load of firewood on her head and pulling a bucket which was half-filled with water. She was nine months pregnant. Sweating profusely, Abike intermittently changed the water-filled bucket from one hand to another, to ease pain. It was a day she wished she was not pregnant. Abike was bending to put the bucket on the floor to rest for a while when she experienced a sharp pain in her abdomen. From experience, she realised with alarm that she was due for delivery. She had a son already. Abike silently prayed, 'Oh God, let it not happen here in the forest with no one to help me.'

The pain subsided a little and she continued trudging her way to the village. At last she arrived with her face wreathed in pain. Abike made efforts to cover the short distance to her hut. Just then a severe pain shot through her tired frame. She screamed. The bucket in her hand and the firewood on her head scattered in different directions as Abike grasped at the nearest tree for support. She was soon surrounded by neighbours who helped her home.

The village 'midwives' did their best to effect safe delivery.

Chief Lamidi Sokoya, Abike's husband, paced to and fro at the back of the house. He had rushed home from the farm when he received the news that his wife was about to deliver.

The last rays of the sun were just disappearing through the sunset when the high-pitched cry of the baby rang out. Within a short time, almost every adult in Yawiri had heard the good news of the safe delivery.

"Eku ewu omo o, Olorun a wo o," was the recurrent greeting coming from well-wishers who had started trooping into Chief Sokoya's compound. The people were congratulating Abike and Lamidi for the safe delivery of the baby and in the same breath prophesying that God will keep the baby safe.

Lamidi smiled with satisfaction. "E se, E se. Thank you," he responded repeatedly.

"Wa un, Wa un," the shrilled cry of the new baby filled the air again. She was a baby girl.

CHAPTER 2: THE NAMING CEREMONY

It was dawn of the eighth day after Abike had given birth. Abike, the baby and some visitors were still sleeping. A wick lantern was burning in a corner of the room. The room was littered with cooking utensils, clothing and farm implements. The sound of mosquitoes buzzing in the air was audible. The baby was lying on a pad of clothes. The shawl meant to cover her had partly slipped off, leaving her half exposed. Abike was snoring. Not too long after, the baby cried. Abike responded almost spontaneously. She was instantly wide awake. She carried the baby and began to breast-feed her. Abike recalled the events of the past eight days with a smile.

"The baby will be circumcised and named today," she mused. "Today is my day of glory." It amused her how her husband's behaviour towards her had changed since the arrival of the baby. It was a positive change. Lamidi, who had been treating her with disrespect, now handled her with queenly courtesy.

'Perhaps it is the new baby,' she thought. 'But it was not so when I gave birth to Tola. Perhaps it is because the new baby is a girl.' Almost instantly she rejected the idea, reasoning that African men hardly treasure girl-children.

Abike could not fathom the reason for Lamidi's change. "Whatever the reason is, I am happy he has changed," she sighed.

The deep voice of Lamidi greeting her suddenly brought her back to reality. Squatting on her knees with the baby still sucking, Abike responded, "e karo oko mi, olowo ori mi," meaning, "good morning my husband and bread winner."

Abike kneeling to greet Lamidi

Sikira and Sidi, Lamidi's nieces were awakened by Lamidi's voice. They arrived the day before for the naming ceremony. They stretched and yawned almost in unison as they knelt to greet Lamidi.

The sun was already filtering through the closed window. A black rat suddenly ran across the room. Lamidi rushed to kill it. Before he could hit the rat, he slipped and fell. Sikira and Sidi found the sight of Lamidi sprawling on the floor funny. However, they managed to suppress a chuckle while muttering, "Sorry uncle," feigning sympathy.

Abike quickly dropped the baby and rushed to her husband's side, asking, "Are you alright?"

"Yes I am, thank you," Lamidi answered. In-between snatches of breath, he continued, "You know the village priest is coming by at 7 a.m. to circumcise the baby. Reverend Olorunda will be here by 7.30 a.m. to name the baby. I want everyone dressed and ready by 6.45 a.m."

He picked his fallen cap from the floor and dusted it. He was almost at the door when he remembered he had not seen the baby. He returned and bent over Abike to look at the face of the child. She was sucking earnestly. He shook the baby's left hand, chuckling. "God has been kind to us in giving us such a beautiful girl," Lamidi whispered. Thereafter, he began to bless the child.

Abike soon realized there was no water for bathing. Someone had to go to the river to fetch water. She pleaded with her in-laws, Sikira and Sidi for assistance. They readily agreed.

Not long after, the sound of empty buckets was heard outside the door. With the baby in her left arm, Abike managed to get to the door. She was still asking, "What happened?" whilst opening the door when she saw her mother-in- law at the door, visibly furious. She had ordered Sikira and Sidi to return the buckets.

"You are nobody's servants," she snapped.

"But mama…" Abike tried to explain.

"Don't 'mama' me," the elderly woman interjected.

"But…" Abike made another effort to explain. She was again cut short.

"Haven't I told you it is an insult for a wife to send her in-laws on errands? Let this be the last time you attempt it."

Abike simply could not take it. "But mama, you know I have just delivered."

Again her mother-in-law interjected her, "And so? Thank God we also had children. We were not trained to ride on our in-laws."

At this point, Ibironke, Abike's junior sister came in. She had just arrived from Ibadan. She heard the latter part of the argument. Without waiting for details or any instruction, she picked up the two buckets and rushed to the river.

By 7.30 a.m. Chief Sokoya's compound was filled with

friends, relatives and well- wishers who had come to grace the occasion of the naming. Few minutes earlier, the village priest had 'circumcised' the baby girl amidst series of incantations and rituals. The poor baby wailed and writhed in pain until Abike had to seal her mouth with breast. Even though Chief Sokoya was a Christian who attended church regularly, like many African men of his time, he believed that the African traditional values and rites should be upheld.

At 7.45am, the pastor of St Peter Anglican Church, a tall elderly man, stood. With eyes surveying the crowd, he remained quiet for some seconds. He naturally commanded respect. There was a hush. Rev Olorunda cleared his throat and said in his characteristic deep voice, "Let us rise and pray." Everyone stood up. The men wearing caps instinctively removed them. After the opening prayer, everyone sat down again.

"You all know why we are gathered here this morning," Rev Olorunda continued. "The purpose is to name this new baby that God has given us. Praise the Lord." The audience responded in unison with a loud, "Hallelujah."

On the table before Rev Olorunda were covered bowls. Some of the bowls contained materials like salt, sugar, money, water, palm-oil, sugar cane, kola-nut, alligator pepper (atare) etc. Also, on the table was a white-leathered Holy Bible.

After a session of dancing and singing praises unto God to express gratitude, Rev Olorunda beckoned the people to be seated. He then gave a short word of exhortation from the Bible saying, "It is God's will that a naming ceremony should be done on the 8th day. We are gathered here today to obey this commandment."

Rev Olorunda took the baby from Abike. While he was adjusting the baby on his left arm, his assistant lifted the bowl containing honey and held it before the Priest. Rev Olorunda dipped the index finger of his right hand into the honey and dropped a little on the baby's tongue. Then he said, "Honey is sweet, baby, your life shall be as sweet as honey."

The people shouted "Amen."

The bowl of honey was replaced with that of salt. Rev Olorunda took a little of the salt and dropped it into the baby's mouth as he prayed, "Salt sweetens, salt preserves, salt flavours, baby, you shall indeed be a salt of the earth. You shall sweeten the life of many generations. Through you, many souls shall be preserved from death and destruction. You shall be a flavour in many people's lives. The good hand of the Lord upon you shall do it in Jesus' name."

The people shouted "Amen" repeatedly.

Following the same pattern, Rev Olorunda used all the items on the table to pray for the baby while the people responded with a loud "Amen." The Reverend was eloquent. Lamidi and Abike were happy. "What are the names of the child?" Rev Olorunda asked, turning to Lamidi and Abike.

Lamidi handed over to the man of God a slip of paper on which he had written some names.

The Reverend silently ran through the names before intoning, "In the name of the Father, the Son and the Holy Ghost, this baby is named Ibironke, Olabisi, Oriade, Omo Sokoya." And the people shouted 'Amen." Thereafter, the Reverend beckoned to the people to repeat the names after him. He offered more prayers on the baby using the meaning of the names.

The naming ceremony was rounded off with eating, drinking and dancing. The traditional drummers, who could hardly wait for Rev. Olorunda to finish, took over the occasion as they beat their drums with gusto. The village of Yawiri was agog with joy.

CHAPTER 3: THE CHILD GROWS

How time flies. It was already seven years since the naming ceremony of Chief Lamidi's daughter. Abike was clad in a wrapper that was barely above her breast. She was sweating profusely as she lifted another bowl of cassava tubers across the compound for shredding. A gust of wind blew across the compound flinging clothes on the drying line in different direction. Abike swore under her breath as she dropped the bowl of cassava tubers she was carrying. She had spent hours washing those clothes. Four dresses had fallen. She picked the fallen clothes one at a time, shaking them in quick successions to remove the sand. Abike dropped the last garment that needed to be re- washed into an empty bowl and returned to carry the bowl of cassava tuber. She was half-way into shredding the cassava when she remembered the promise she gave Mama Sikira. 'I must return Mama Sikira's money today by all means,' she muttered.

Abike in wrapper shredding cassava

Abike recollected with shame how three months earlier she had literally gone on her knees to beg Mama Sikira to release two bowls of beans on credit. There was no grain in the house to eat then. Lamidi couldn't give her money for food for close to six months. There was drought in Yawiri for over one year. All the plants were fast drying up. But for the recent gift of one thousand naira from her nephew in Lagos, Mama Sikira would have further disgraced her. "Bisiiiii," Abike called.

Bisi was the baby named seven years earlier. Somehow, Lamidi and Abike could not have another child after that. Though Bisi had several other names, the name 'Bisi' stuck with her. Meanwhile, Bisi was busy building sand towers in the next house. She had just raised her hand to beat her friend Titi for breaking one of her sand towers, when she heard the mother's shrill voice calling her.

"Bisi, where are you?" Abike called again.

"I am here, in Titi's house," Bisi answered and ran towards her mother. Fear crept into her sweat-dripping pretty face. She feared Abike. She had received several beatings from her for being too playful. Bisi therefore preferred being with Lamidi, her father. Lamidi allowed Bisi to play for hours unchecked. 'What offence have I committed now?' Bisi thought, noticing her mum's look of anger. "Mama, here I am," Bisi said.

"How many times have I told you not to go to that house again?" Abike dipped her right hand under her wrapper and bought out some money from her waist band. She counted it slowly and loudly "eni, eji, eta … ogorun, one, two, three … one hundred. Here is one hundred naira (N100), run and give it to mama Sikira in her shop. Make sure you don't stop anywhere to play, you hear?"

"Yes Mama," Bisi replied. She curtseyed [bowing slightly at the knees] as she took the money from her mother. With a sigh of relief, she sped off.

The sight that met her when she got to the market was

unusual. A large crowd of people in a circle had their attention riveted on a captivating event. Once in a while, the crowd bellowed with excitement. Though Bisi could not see the event that had engrossed the crowd, she could hear the throbbing sound of the African talking drums, the sonorous voice of a singer and what sounded like the pounding footsteps of some dancers. Curiosity got the better side of the little girl. Without any thought of her mother's warning, she pressed her way into crowd. At last she found herself in front of the crowd. It was then she saw it was the village magician performing again.

Bisi was deeply fascinated by the display. Apparently, she had witnessed the scene many times before, but she could hardly be tired of watching it. She settled down to enjoy the spectacle. Presently the magician was running a long knife over his bare stomach.

The village magician running a knife through his stomach

He was trying to cut himself. Apparently, because of the charms used or due to the effect of his magic, or both, the seemingly sharp knife could not cut into the magician's flesh. He paused, looked towards a young man in the crowd and with delight etched on his sweaty face, he made a few deft strokes in the air with his knife as if to say, 'see, this knife is useless against my flesh.' He then beckoned to the young man and instructed him to use the knife to slaughter a fowl that was tied to a stone nearby. The young man obeyed. At the touch of the knife, the fowl's head was cut off. The fowl cried and jerked for some time before dying? There was a mystified silence. The magician collected the knife back and cleaned it. He gave it to the young man again. This time he instructed him to use the knife on his stomach. Without any expression of fear, the young man obeyed again. With all the strength he could muster, he tried cutting the Magician's stomach with the sharp knife. His effort proved abortive. The crowd cheered as the drummers increased the intensity of their drums. The whole atmosphere was charged with excitement.

Bisi was mesmerized. She recollected the pain she felt some time ago when she mistakenly cut her finger with a penknife. She was still wondering on the magical performance when she remembered her mother's warning and the errand she had sent her to do. Reluctantly, she began to squeeze her way back through the crowd. Sensing she had lost some time, she ran to Mama Sikira's shop.

She was panting when she got to Mama Sikira's stall. She had begun to deliver her mother's message when she realised the N100 was missing. Bisi felt cold. She lifted her gown and searched for the money.

"What happened? Did you stop somewhere?" Mama Sikira asked.

"I...I...," Bisi stammered and began to sob. "Why don't you trace your way back through the route you took to this place?

Perhaps it dropped on the way while you were running," mama Sikira suggested.

Slowly tracing her steps back to the house, Bisi kept searching along the road in between sobs and tears, fervently hoping she would find the money before getting home.

'What will I tell mama now?' Bisi was terrified. At last, she got home without finding the money. Bisi felt like running away from the house rather than face her mum. She was still contemplating what to do when Abike came out from the house and saw her crying.

"What is the matter Bisi? Did someone beat you? Have you lost the money? Come on speak up," Abike snapped.

"I, I ... lost the money," Bisi managed to mutter.

"You did what?" Abike flared up. Almost hysterically, Abike began to beat Bisi while cursing her at the same time. "Olosi, Olori-buruku ... Omo- alaigboran. Stupid senseless, stubborn child."

Bisi covered her face with both arms and screamed for help. Within minutes, Lamidi's compound was filled with concerned neighbours. Abike was on top of Bisi, slapping and hitting simultaneously. It took four persons to drag Abike off Bisi.

Neighbours dragging Abike while beating Bisi

"Abba, se o fe paa ni? Do you want to kill her?" the concerned neighbours shouted.

"Yes, let me kill the foolish girl," Abike retorted angrily.

"What has she done?" someone asked.

"Who does not know how Mama Sikira has disgraced me in this village over the money I owed her? And who does not know the financial hardship we have been through in the village? Only yesterday I received a gift of money. It was small but I had to squeeze Mama Sikira's money out of it. That was the money this stupid girl threw away while watching the village magician." Abike charged at Bisi again.

Two neighbours that were nearby stopped her.

One angry neighbour shouted at Abike, "Abike what on earth is wrong with you. Do you want to kill your child because of N100? Have you forgotten so soon what you went through to get her?" The neighbour angrily took Bisi's hand and handed her over to Abike, "Kill her, if that is what you want."

Like a blazing fire doused with water, Abike instantly calmed down. She was ashamed for causing so much scene over nothing as her neighbour had rightly observed. With a sober voice, Abike thanked her neighbours for their intervention. She then drew Bisi to her side, wiping her tears with her wrapper.

CHAPTER 4: SCHOOL NOT FOR GIRLS

There had been no drop of rain for close to one year in Yawiri and the environs. Lamidi and other elders in the village had tried everything they knew how to do to induce rain in the land. Presently, they were preparing for another ritual which involved human sacrifice. Lamidi was getting tired of the sacrifices.

"Why on earth haven't the sacrifices brought rain all these months?" he reasoned. "I can't continue sitting like this. I must do something. My family is suffering." He stood up picking his hoe and cutlass. He made up his mind to till the ground and plant anyhow, rain or no rain.

"I'll dig a well on the farm and use the water to wet the plant morning and evening. It is hard work, but what else can I do?"

Sweating profusely under the intense heat, Lamidi began to dig mounds in the hard ground. At intervals, he paused to take a sip of palm-wine that his friend Baba Fatai had given him. Lamidi was on the sixth mound when he realized it was getting dark. It takes about two hours of brisk walk to get to the village. He told himself it was time to leave. It was 8 pm when he got home.

Abike, Bisi and Tola were sitting outside when he arrived. In unison, they got up to welcome him. "Ekabo. Welcome." He responded, "Ekule. Meet you well in the house."

Abike went into the kitchen. She came back with a bowl of water and gave it to Lamidi, kneeling slightly as she did so. Lamidi literally gulped the water. After a tedious day at work, he was hungry, thirsty and tired. While returning the empty bowl to the kitchen, Abike said over her shoulder, "There is water in the bathroom. And your food is on the table."

Lamidi was very pleased with Abike. He still could not comprehend how she managed to keep food on the table, even though he was not able to give her money for house-keeping for many months now. The interesting thing was that she never complained either. Lamidi thanked God for giving him such an understanding wife.

As he was heading for the bathroom with a wrapper tied round his waist, he noticed that Bisi was unusually quiet. It was quite unlike her. He walked back towards her, bent down and asked, "Bisi what is wrong? Why are you so quiet?"

Tola, Bisi's brother, responded, "Baba, she wants to go school. I have been teaching her A, B, C and 1, 2, 3"

Bisi has been worrying him for some time now about wanting to go to school. She simply couldn't understand why she would not be allowed to attend school like Tola and other children in the village. Bisi began to sob. Lamidi pacified her, "Don't cry Bisi. How many times am I going to tell you that school is not necessary for girls? When you marry, you would take care of your children and the home. Your husband would take care of your needs."

Bisi refused to accept this explanation. She cried the more while shrugging her shoulders in protest, "Baba, please send me to school. Girls go to school. I heard it from Baba Fatai's radio."

"Oh, I see! Is that where you have been filling your head with these strange ideas? School is probably okay for city girls, but not for villagers like us, do you understand?" Bisi refused to accept her dad's explanation.

Lamidi stood wondering if he had made the right decision. He also wondered whether his decision not to send Bisi to school was not more of financial reason than cultural belief.

"Whatever the reason," he reassured himself, "it is a sheer waste of money and time sending a girl to school only for her to end up in the kitchen and nursing babies."

Lamidi went to take his bath. He could still hear Bisi sobbing as he entered the bathroom. Worried, he thought, 'What on earth am I going to do now seeing this girl is so determined?'

CHAPTER 5: TRIP TO THE CITY

Lamidi had travelled to the city of Ibadan, the capital city of Oyo state, Nigeria, to cash a cheque of twenty thousand naira that his friend gave him three weeks earlier. He did not understand what the paper enclosed with the letter meant until the boy who read the letter explained the procedure for turning the paper into money.

Lamidi had been standing by the ring-road expressway for almost thirty minutes in the bid to cross the road to the bank. He could not understand why the vehicles were moving so fast. "Why for heaven's sake can't they stop briefly for people to cross?" Lamidi asked for the umpteenth time. "Kai! Crossing this road is another work altogether. This is why I hate coming to the city," Lamidi moaned.

The road suddenly became quiet with no visible sign of car passing. 'This is my chance,' Lamidi thought. With one hand wrapping his 'agbada' (an overflowing gown) tightly around his body and the other hand holding his cap to his head, Lamidi ran across the road. He was in the middle of the road when he suddenly heard the screeching sound of tyres. Turning, he saw a car stopping about a hair's breadth of his leg. Lamidi screamed for help, throwing his arms into the air. A sudden gust of wind blew off his cap. It was a scene. Within moments, passers-by came to his aid. They retrieved his cap and helped him cross the road. At last, Lamidi got inside Union Bank.

Lamidi trying to cross express road at Ibadan

"The next hurdle now is how to turn this paper into money," he pondered. Lamidi was still wondering, and in the state of confusion when a young girl who had come to the bank to deposit money observed he needed help. "Baba, kile fe? What do you want Daddy?"

Replying, Lamidi showed her the cheque and said, "I want to change this paper to money." The young girl took Lamidi to the 'Inquiry Desk.' After cross-examination, the inquiry clerk found that Lamidi needed to open a bank account since the cheque was crossed. The clerk led Lamidi to the Bank Manager.

"Sit down, Baba," the Manager, a young lady of about thirty beckoned Lamidi to a seat after scrutinizing the cheque. The lady took her time to explain the banking procedure to Lamidi. She eventually offered to help by paying the cheque into a special account while the bank advanced him the money. She, however, warned Lamidi not to expect the same favor in future as it was completely against banking protocol. Lamidi was full of appreciation.

"Thank you very much madam, God bless you."

Lamidi was impressed by the conduct of the Manager. 'It is almost unthinkable, that a lady could be in such a highly placed position, with so many men under her control. I have never seen anything like this before. So, this is what going to school can do.'

It suddenly dawned on Lamidi that he had made a mistake in not allowing Bisi to attend school. 'Oh, how I wish Bisi will be like this woman. Bisi must attend school by all means. Thank God I came to the city to witness this. And thank God this money came at a time like this. Now, I have something to pay her school fees.'

Lamidi could hardly wait for the bus to get to Yawiri village. Yes! Bisi must go to school.

CHAPTER 6: BISI GOING TO SCHOOL?

It was 5 p.m. when Lamidi got to Yawiri. The journey took a long time, not so much for the distance but for the rough road and the old vehicle that conveyed them.

"Baba, Baba, welcome," Bisi and Tola shouting, ran to welcome Lamidi as he alighted from the lorry. Lamidi was visibly tired, having been cramped with four other hefty men in a space meant for three persons for over four hours. The joyful sight of the children running towards him however revived him. Smiling, he bent to pick the children in turn for a 'throw.' Bisi screamed with delight coupled with fear as Lamidi released her into the air.

As they walked towards the house, Bisi asked, "Baba, what did you buy for us?"

"Yes, Baba, you promised to buy something for us," Tola reiterated.

"I remember. I bought biscuits for you," Lamidi responded.

"Biscuits, Biscuit," Tola and Bisi chanted and leaped with excitement.

While Lamidi was searching for the biscuits, Abike came into the room carrying a bucket of water. After putting down the bucket, she knelt to welcome her husband.

"Welcome Baba Bisi. How was your trip?"

"It was fine. But I have learnt a few lessons," Lamidi said wryly.

"What lessons?" Abike asked as she walked towards the kitchen. She returned with a cup of water for Lamidi. Lamidi took a sip of the water and placed the cup on the table by his side.

He patted the seat beside him, "Sit down Abike, we must discuss the issue of Bisi going to school."

"Bisi going to school? Have you changed your mind then?" Abike responded with excitement. She had secretly wished Lamidi would allow Bisi to attend school. 'This must be an answered prayer,' Abike thought. Bisi, who had been struggling to open her biscuit overheard her parents' discussion. She couldn't hold herself. She began to chant …

"I am going to school. I am going to school."

"Okay, okay, Bisi, let's have some silence. I am discussing with your mother," Lamidi interrupted Bisi.

Bisi, still visibly excited, kept quiet and sat close to Lamidi, looking expectantly into his face.

"Abike, the trip to the city has opened my eyes. I have learnt some lessons. Now I know it is good and indeed necessary for girls to attend school." Lamidi then narrated his encounter with the lady Manager he met at Union Bank, Ibadan.

"Baba Bisi, you mean a woman was controlling all the men, even the married men in the bank?" Abike inquired with surprise. It sounded like a fairy tale. It was an abomination in Yoruba land for the voice of a woman to be heard in public gathering, not to talk of controlling men. It is strange and unimaginable. 'But then, Baba Bisi cannot be lying,' she reasoned.

Lamidi's deep voice interrupted her thoughts. "That was exactly what I saw. Because she was more educated than the men in the bank, she was made their head. That is what education does, it makes you the head," Lamidi, with an air of the wise, lectured Abike.

"If education does such wonders, then Bisi too must go to school. I want her to be the head in her working place like that woman," Abike said excitedly.

"That is why I am discussing all this with you. Tomorrow, I am taking her to school," Lamidi declared with a note of finality.

Bisi could no longer hold herself. She ran to her brother to announce the good news, "Tola, Tola, I am going to school tomorrow."

Tola rejoiced with Bisi. He had been Bisi's secret teacher for quite some time now.

"But there is one thing," Lamidi caught everyone's attention. "Bisi, when you start attending school, you must promise me you will do all your household chores before going to school each day - sweep the floor, feed the chicken and goat and wash the plates in the kitchen, and do the other works you do every morning, okay?"

"Baba, you know I am not lazy. I'll do all my chores before going to school every morning," Bisi reassured her father.

After supper, Lamidi stretched out on the reclining chair that he inherited from his grandfather. As he watched his wife and children clearing the plates used, an overwhelming sense of peace and joy flooded his heart.

"I know it is the right thing to do. Even though it is against tradition, but I will stick out my neck to break tradition on this issue."

Bisi was still excited. She was running after Tola towards the kitchen when Lamidi spoke. "It's all right children. You need to sleep early so you can wake early for school tomorrow, okay?"

With exchanges of goodnight, everyone went to bed. Bisi kept feeling it was daybreak already. She wondered why the time was suddenly so slow to pass. She could hardly wait to get to school. At last, a cock crowed. Bisi tapped her mother and whispered. "Mama, it is daybreak. Let's get up."

"Ummm..." Abike grunted and turned over. After some few minutes she resumed snoring. Bisi knew if she persisted in waking her mother, she might incur her wrath. She tip-toed into the kitchen to begin her chores.

"Where on earth is that match box?" She muttered angrily under her breath. Her hand suddenly hit a bowl and it fell on the floor, making a loud bang that literally woke everyone.

"Bisi, what are you doing there? It is still a long while before day. What have you broken there?" Abike asked.

"I … I have not broken anything. I want to start my chores. I don't want to get to school late," Bisi sheepishly replied.

"Oh, come on, you still have a lot of time to complete your chores and still get to school early. Come back to bed." Abike chided.

With the shrug of her shoulders, Bisi answered, "Mama, I can't sleep any longer. I'll rather begin my chores now."

"Abike allow her. We all get excited with new experiences," Lamidi interjected from his room.

Bisi eventually found the matches, lit the wick-lamp and set to work. In less than one hour, she had completed her chores. Thereafter, she took her bath and was all dressed ready for school as early as 5 am.

With nothing else to do Bisi decided to relax on her father's reclining chair. Within a short time, she nodded off and began to dream.

She was in school. The boys were playing football, while some of the girls were skipping. It was her turn to skip. As she moved to enter the rope, another girl, a senior student, barged in and pushed her off. Bisi protested, "No, no, no, it is my turn, no, no ... that was the expression on her lips as Abike woke her up.

"Bisi, Bisi..." Abike gently shook Bisi. "It is time for school. Get up."

Bisi stretched and yawned. She could hardly believe she was not yet in school. The dream was so real.

"Mama, are we not going to school again?" Bisi anxiously inquired.

"You are going. Your dad will be taking you to school. He will soon be ready."

"But he has not taken his bath," Bisi observed.

"Don't worry my daughter. It's your first day at school anyway. Moreover, you have not taken your breakfast. While you are doing that, your father will be ready." Abike re-assured Bisi.

At last Lamidi was ready. "Won't you eat? Your food is ready," Abike asked him.

"Don't worry I will eat when I get back. We are getting late," Lamidi responded. "Bisi, let's go. Where is Tola?"

"He has gone to school. You know they punish those who get to school late," Abike explained. Lamidi nodded, took Bisi's hand and proceeded to St. Peter Primary School, Yawiri.

Bisi was elated. "At last I am going to school. I pray it is not a dream this time around," she muttered.

CHAPTER 7: BISI IN SCHOOL

The white background of the big sign-board with the words *'St Peter Primary School, Yawiri'* reflected the sun rays on Lamidi's eyes as he came out of the last turning to the school. Instinctively, he shielded his eyes with his right hand while wiping his sweaty face with a brown dirty apron he used as handkerchief. The temperature was high as usual. He heaved a sigh of relief as they entered the cool of the shade formed by the cluster of trees lining the road leading to the school.

It was a beautiful and well-kept school. St. Peter was one of the schools the Christian Missionaries established when they came to the area.

The school bell rang. It was the bell for general assembly. The pupils walking along with Lamidi and Bisi spontaneously began to run towards the assembly. They dreaded the punishment for latecomers: It was either six strokes of cane or fetching six buckets of water from the stream. The pupils found both punishments gruesome. Bisi, already feeling like one of them, unconsciously attempted to run too, but for Lamidi's restraining hand.

"This is your first day in school. You need to register first," Lamidi explained to her. So, they found their way to the headmaster's office. The headmaster was preparing to go to the assembly when Lamidi and Bisi entered his office.

"Good morning, Mr. Thomas," Lamidi stretched his hand for a handshake while Bisi knelt.

The headmaster bowed his head as mark of respect to the chief, while shaking Chief Lamidi Sokoya. "Good morning, Chief Sokoya. It is a surprise seeing you after a long while. How can I help you sir?"

"Yes, you can. I have decided that Bisi should begin schooling."

There was a mixed expression of surprise, joy and respect on the headmaster's face. Surprise because it was almost a tug of war convincing parents in the area to send their daughters to school. Even a recent law enacted stipulating a harsh penalty to parents who refused to send their daughters to school could not intimidate them. And here is Chief Sokoya, one of the chief defenders of the tradition voluntarily bringing his daughter to school. It was a pleasant surprise.

"Chief Sokoya, this is good news to me. I will attend to you shortly. Please wait for me here while I quickly give a word to the students at the assembly. Have your seat please."

The wall clock was chiming eight o'clock when he returned. "Sorry to keep you waiting Chief Sokoya. The admission process will be over in no time." He walked briskly to the shelf of files at the east end of his fairly large office. Flipping through the files on the 3rd rung, he found the file on admissions. He pulled it out and returned to his seat. He brought out a blank admission form from the file and began to question Lamidi.

"What are her names?"

"Ibironke, Olabisi, Ayinke, Osuolale, Oluwayem…."

Mr. Thomas interrupted him. "This is enough Chief. We have to select only two of those names. The space in our forms can't take more than three names at a time. Which two names do you prefer for her?"

Lamidi was silent for some time whilst thinking.

At last he spoke up. "If that is the case, then record Olabisi Ibironke Sokoya as her school names."

"That is good. And how old is she?"

"Eight years and two months."

"The mother's name…"

"Abike Sokoya"

After taking the relevant information on Olabisi Sokoya, Mr. Thomas inspected the completed form with satisfaction. Finally, he announced:

"The only thing remaining now is her passport photograph, and of course her books and school uniform."

He pulled out the lower drawer of his table and picked out a sheet of paper. It was the list of the items for new students. He gave it to Chief Sokoya.

"Chief Sokoya, here is the list of books and other items you must buy for Bisi. The school fees are one thousand five hundred naira for this term."

Lamidi collected the form. Though he could not read, he decided he would give it to his neighbour's son, who normally read letters for him. Out of curiosity he asked, "Mr. Thomas, are you not having the books and uniform here in school? I could just pay for the items."

"The school uniform is available but not the books. Give me a minute." Mr. Thomas walked to the adjoining room and called:

"Mrs. Akinyemi, kindly spare a minute."

A tall dark pretty woman in her late thirties stood up at the far corner of the teachers' common room and came into the Headmaster's office.

Mr. Thomas introduced the Teacher, "Chief Lamidi, meet Mrs. Doja Akinyemi."

Lamidi stood up and shook her hands, "I am pleased to meet you madam."

"I am pleased to meet you sir," Doja replied with a bright smile, bending at the knee as a mark of respect.

Mr. Thomas continued, "Chief Sokoya is Bisi's father. She is about to commence schooling. Do you have a uniform that could fit her?" Mrs. Akinyemi sized up Bisi, "We have only two left. Let me try them on her."

Taking Bisi by the hand, Mrs. Akinyemi took her into an adjoining room. She opened a cupboard and brought out some school uniforms. The first uniform Bisi tried fitted her so well Mrs. Akinyemi could not but exclaim. Turning her around while admiring her, she said to Bisi, "Ain't you lucky? The dress fits

31

you perfectly. And you are looking good in it. Now, let's return to Mr. Thomas."

"Chief Sokoya, you've got a pretty daughter there," Mr. Thomas remarked as Bisi returned with Mrs. Akinyemi. Lamidi smiled. Bisi has been special to him, right from birth. He felt so proud of her.

"So how much is the uniform? Lamidi asked.

Mr. Thomas turned to Mrs. Akinyemi for a response. "It is three hundred naira, sir."

"And the school fees, how much?"

"One thousand five hundred naira," Mr. Thomas answered.

Lamidi proudly brought out a fat ward of currency notes and counted the amount. From the corner of his eyes, he noticed he was making an impression on Mrs. Akinyemi. After counting, he gave the money to the headmaster who immediately passed it to Mrs. Akinyemi and requested her to issue receipts for the payments.

Lamidi reflected, "It is really good to have money. Some few months back, I could hardly afford one hundred Naira. And come to think of it, education is not too expensive after all. To think that I have deprived my daughter of education for such a flimsy excuse for so long. Thank God, it is better late than never."

While waiting for the receipt, Mr Thomas, who had been itching to know the reason for Chief Sokoya's sudden change of attitude, asked him, "Chief Sokoya, you took me completely by surprise with this decision to allow Bisi to attend school. Everyone in this village knew you to be a hardline antagonist of the idea of sending girls to school. What really happened?"

"It happened when I went to Ibadan to collect the money my friend sent to me …" Thus Chief Sokoya recounted his encounter with the bank lady Manager who assisted him few days earlier. "You see, that was the turning point. This woman so affected me that I decided there and then that Bisi too must become great like that woman, hence, I made the decision to send her to school contrary to our tradition."

"This is a fantastic story, almost like what you read in books. I congratulate you sir on this wise decision you have taken." Mr. Thomas remarked, "We shall do what we can to ensure your daughter learns fast to make up for the lost years. If she learns fast, she can even be given accelerated promotion."

Excited with the idea of double promotion, Lamidi exclaimed, "Really? That sounds so nice Mr. Thomas, can you advise me on how best I can help Bisi to achieve this feat?"

Mr. Thomas paused for moment thinking. He suddenly snapped his index finger and thumb together as an idea popped into his mind. "What? Mrs. Doja Akinyemi here is the person that can help you. Apart from being an experienced teacher, she has desired to find a pupil to give private teaching lessons. Talk to her, she will definitely help you."

Just then Mrs. Akinyemi returned and gave the receipt to Mr. Thomas who passed it to Chief Sokoya. Mr. Thomas turned to Mrs. Akinyemi.

"Mrs. Akinyemi, please take Bisi to Mr. Ogedenge, the primary 1B teacher. She is to be in that class for the time being. Please come back to my office when you are done. Chief has a proposition to discuss with you."

She was surprised. 'What on earth could a whole Chief want to discuss with me,' she thought. She could hardly wait for the information. She quickly took the new intake and headed for primary 1B. Bisi waved to her father.

School had started in full swing for Bisi. She discovered she liked this lady teacher who has been conducting her around. She wished she were in her class. There was a dead silence in the school premises as students were busy learning in all the classes. Once in a while, the sound of a vehicle passing through Yawiri's only motor way could be heard in the background.

"Aunty, am I going to be in your class?"

"No, my girl. But don't worry, you will like your teacher as well. He is a good teacher."

Presently they were in class 1B. As Mrs. Akinyemi entered with Bisi, all the students rose and chanted in unison,

"Gooooooood moooooorning ma."

"Good morning students, how are you?" "

We are fine, thank you ma, and you?"

"I am fine too, thank you. Please sit down."

Mrs. Akinyemi walked up to Mr. Titus Ogedengbe who had just turned from the chalkboard.

"Good morning Mr. Ogedengbe. Here is a new pupil for you. Her name is Bisi. The headmaster said you should introduce her to the class and give her the necessary induction. I will see you later."

Out of eagerness to know what Chief Sokoya wanted to tell her, Mrs. Akinyemi sped back to the headmaster's office.

Meanwhile, Mr. Ogedengbe introduced Bisi to the class and gave her a seat.

In unison, the class chorused, "Welcome Bisi. God bless you."

Bisi did not know how to respond in English. "Oooo," she responded in Yoruba Language.

The whole class burst into laughter. Bisi was embarrassed. The teacher quickly came to her aid. "Why are you laughing? Were you not all like her when you came six months ago? Remember she is a new pupil. We are all here to learn. No one should laugh at each other's mistake, okay?"

"Okay sir," they all responded

"Now, let's continue our lesson on A, B, C."

Using the boldly written alphabets on the chalkboard, Mr. Ogedengbe directed the pupils to repeat after him....

"hay"   "hay"

"bee"   "bee"

"cee"   "cee"...

"zed"   "zed"

Chief Sokoya was laughing heartily in response to a statement made by Mr. Thomas when Mrs. Akinyemi returned.

"Well, well ... Mrs Akinyemi, Chief Sokoya wants to know if it will be convenient for you to start giving his children extra lessons. He desired accelerated promotion for Bisi."

Mrs. Akinyemi was excited. This is what she had wanted. Without much thinking, she blurted.

"Yes sir, it is convenient."

Thereafter, the agreement as per charges and periods for the extra lesson was reached.

Chief Sokoya was happy. He rose, thanked Mr. Thomas and Mrs. Akinyemi for their benevolence and returned to his house with a smile on his weather-beaten face.

CHAPTER 8: THE ILLICIT AFFAIR

Abike had travelled to take care of her sick mother. She had gone for more than a week. Lamidi had missed her terribly. The children were too young to take care of themselves. And he was simply not used to cooking. Presently, he was pacing to and fro thinking of what the children would eat when they return from school.

An idea suddenly popped into his mind, "Mrs. Akinyemi, the lesson teacher, can assist with cooking." She is due to come for her lessons. For reasons he could not explain, Lamidi got excited with the idea. Doja, as he now fondly calls her, can be excused from teaching today. "I simply can't go to the village market," he muttered. He had barely reached this conclusion, when Tola and Bisi arrived from school and greeted, "Baba ... meet you well." Tola prostrated while Bisi knelt on the floor.

"Welcome, my dear children," Lamidi responded with a wide smile while patting them on the back.

Sitting them down, he inquired what they had learnt for the day. Bisi would hardly allow Tola to speak. She was already reading A, B, C to Z fluently and could count up to 100 in less than 2 months. Mrs. Akinyemi, their private teacher, has been doing a wonderful job. What really helped the exercise was that Bisi was quite intelligent. She learnt so fast it amazed everyone.

"Before your teacher comes, go to the kitchen. There is gari (fried grated cassava) in the cupboard. At the top right-hand corner, you will also see a 'tinko' (dried meat). You are taking soaked 'gari' with 'tinko' this afternoon. When Aunty Doja comes, she will help us cook a better meal."

The children were happy. They rushed to the kitchen and did as their father had directed.

Tola and Bisi had finished eating. While waiting for their private teacher, they both nodded off.

Not long after, the weather changed. The sky became dark

whilst the storm brewed. Leaves, clothes, dust were all in the air. Some roofs were almost getting ripped off. Lamidi rushed to close all the windows. He then carried Tola and Bisi into their room, making them more comfortable on the mat. It was raining already. He was about to lock the main door into the house when he heard running feet and a frantic knock on the door.

"Who is that?" He inquired. "It is me sir, Doja."

He had almost forgotten, the private teacher! Of course, he was expecting the lady to come so she could help do some shopping and cooking. But alas, this rain wouldn't allow that. He opened the door to let her in. Doja was drenched with rain. The rain was quite unexpected. She had not taken her umbrella. The dress she wore also showed her unpreparedness. She wore a flimsy, almost transparent blouse. With the rain that had beaten her, the transparent blouse had stuck to her body.

Lamidi forgot himself for a brief moment whilst staring. Ideas began to fly around in his head. For a minute, he did not know exactly how he could help her. At last, he mumbled, still gaping, "Sorry you are so wet. You must change. The only thing I can think of now is one of Mama Tola's wrappers. You can use that while you put off your wet dress to dry. By the time you are ready to go, it should be dry."

"Thank you, sir, but I will manage," Doja responded, reluctant to accept the offer.

However, when the cold began to bite harder, she changed her mind and accepted the offer. Lamidi handed her one of his wife's wrappers. She entered one of the rooms to change.

Lamidi could no longer control himself. Of course, he had secretly been admiring Doja for some time now. But then, he had been dimissing the idea, 'How can a married man with two children do such a thing? Moreover, the lady is married too.' But under the present circumstance, Chief Lamidi Sokoya appeared to have lost all sense of morality.

"This is my chance," he muttered with excitement. "Mama

Tola has travelled, and the children are fast asleep."

The only thing pricking his conscience was the thought that Doja was married. He knew it was dangerous having an affair with a married woman, particularly in Yawiri. He, however, threw caution to the winds.

'It is raining and dark already, no one will know,' he reassured himself. With caution thrown to the winds, he hatched a plan. 'Since it is cold, I'll offer her schnapps alcoholic drink until she gets slightly drunk, then I'll take my chance.'

Just then, Doja came out of the room with the wrapper tied above her breasts. It was apparent that she had nothing else on underneath. Lamidi could no longer hold himself. He felt an irresistible force pulling him towards Doja.

Doja could sense Lamidi's feelings. 'But what can I do in this situation?' She reasoned. 'I can only pray that we shall both control ourselves.'

The rain was not helping matters either. Rather than abate, it increased in intensity. The wrapper could not keep her warm any longer, she was visibly shivering.

'Why on earth have I come to this place at this time,' she thought frantically.

Seeing her shivering, Lamidi offered her a seat and said as calmly as he could, "Doja, I can see you are cold and shivering. I have schnapps. It should keep you warm." Without waiting for her response, he went into his room and brought out the schnapps drink with two cups. He drew a stool close to Doja and poured out the drink, filling the cup to the brim.

Doja reluctantly collected it, thanked Lamidi and took a sip. She thought, "I'll take a little and leave the rest. I must be careful not to get drunk." But alas, the more she took a sip, the warmer and better she felt. She could hardly explain what was happening to her. It was as if with each passing second, her willpower for self-control and caution was being thrown to the winds. She simply couldn't stop herself from taking one more sip. As the alcoholic drink began to take its toll on Doja, she found herself desiring Chief Sokoya. She knew he liked her. She knew his wife had travelled. She knew the children were fast asleep. And her husband had travelled. This awareness coupled with the effect of the drink further made her vulnerable. She could hardly put up any resistance by the time Chief Sokoya made a pass at her.

Thus, began an illicit affair between Chief Sokoya and Mrs. Doja Akinyemi. Doja returned to her house 5 am the following morning before people began to wake up. She felt no regret for what had happened. To her surprise, she found herself looking forward to another time with Chief Sokoya. Doja could hardly explain her feelings. It was as if she had become a slave to her body. She felt like someone possessed, literally driven by a force beyond her control. All she knew was that her passion for Chief Sokoya was growing by the day, even when her husband had returned from his trip.

CHAPTER 9: BISI EXCELS IN SCHOOL

Bisi screamed with joy. She could hardly believe her eyes. She read the headmaster's comment again. "Bisi has performed excellently. She has been given double promotion to Primary 5." She clasped the report sheet to her chest and danced in circles. It was the second time she had received double promotion in two years. It was almost unbelievable. Some of her friends gathered around her rejoicing with her, while some of her classmates were jealous.

The school had just closed for the session. Bisi hurriedly packed her books and materials from her school desk and dumped them into her school bag. She was too excited to care about arranging things. "I must not miss seeing Aunty Doja," she muttered while rushing towards the spot she was sure to see her. In the process, one of her books dropped onto the floor without her awareness. She was almost out of the classroom when she heard her name being called by Tope her classmate.

"Bisi, Bisi … your book has dropped."

She retraced her steps, picked the book and said, "Thank you." She hurriedly forced the book into her overloaded bag and dashed out of the classroom. She knew exactly where Aunty Doja would be at this time. For some time now, she had been staying in the school library, except when some students were using the library. Bisi ran there.

"Aunty, Auntie," Bisi's high pitched voice rang through the small library with excitement. There was nobody in the library. She ran into the small inner room where Doja normally sat. The room was empty.

"Oh, where could Aunty be? She must see my result. It is Aunty Doja who has made this double promotion possible. Oh, where is Aunty now?" Bisi frantically thought while searching the room for any sign that Doja was still around. Suddenly, she spotted her handbag on the floor behind the desk. Her hope rose.

She knew Aunty Doja couldn't be far because the bag contains her valuables. As she got out of the room to go searching for her, Doja came into the Library. Bisi screamed with joy.

"Aunty, Aunty… see, see," frantically searching through her bag, she brought out the examination report. "I have been given another double promotion." With a wide smile on her face, Doja carried Bisi's shoulders high before clasping her to her bosom. Bisi instinctively twinned her legs around Doja's waist.

"You have done extremely well, my daughter though I am not too surprised. You are truly a brilliant child. Well done. You have made me proud."

And with that, Doja tenderly put Bisi down while putting her right hand around her neck. Doja sat down and placed Bisi on her laps. Over the last two years, especially since she had fallen in love with Lamidi, she discovered she had grown to love Bisi so much like her own daughter. Perhaps this was further facilitated by the fact that she had no child of her own, five years after marriage. The problem had been with her husband. This had made Doja despise and loathe him, more so after meeting Lamidi. While fondling Bisi's hair, Doja wondered, 'How I wish I was married to Lamidi. How I wish Bisi was my daughter.'

In a flash, she recalled how Lamidi had passionately made love to her the last time they met in their secret meeting place. It is a wonder no-one had discovered the illicit affair so far. Doja held Bisi closer to her body.

Bisi felt loved. "My mother has never loved me like Aunty Doja. Mama was always shouting at me over every little mistake," Bisi thought.

This perhaps explained why Bisi had grown so fond of Doja. Pathetically, it appears Doja was succeeding in 'stealing both husband and daughter' from Abike by the day.

Abike seemed not to be aware of what was going on. She was rather full of praise and appreciation for 'Aunty Doja, our dear teacher,' as she fondly called her. Abike often went to the extent of preparing lunch for Doja every day she was in the house to teach the children extra lessons. As she recollected these episodes, Doja shuddered, suddenly feeling cold, though the atmosphere was far from cold.

She dreaded the day she and Lamidi would be discovered and exposed. Presently, she felt Bisi should begin to go home. Only few students were left in school.

"Okay, Bisi, it's time to go home."

"Let me stay with you, Auntie, please," Bisi pleaded.

"No, it's getting late. Your parents will be getting worried. And remember you are going home alone today. Holiday has started so we are having a break from extra lessons also, Okay?"

"Okay Aunty." With that, Bisi stood up, picked her bag and waved to Doja.

Doja waved back with a smile. As Bisi was about to get out of the library door, Doja said, "Bisi, come to my house for a visit on Sunday afternoon, will you? Tell mummy and daddy, I am sure they'll allow you to come. I'll prepare a delicious meal for you, for doing so well in your exams."

Bisi was thrilled with the invitation. She ran back to Doja and hugged her. "Thank you, Aunty. I can't wait for Sunday to come."

Finally, almost reluctantly, they parted.

CHAPTER 10: THE MYSTERIOUS BLACK THREAD

Segun Akinyemi, Doja's husband, had just returned from the fetish priest. He could no longer bear the thought that his wife was having an affair with another man. Though there was no evidence yet, everything pointed to the speculation. Doja's movement and conduct had been suspicious in recent times. She wouldn't allow Segun to make love to her for weeks on end, and if she did, it was without emotional expressions. She could not be bothered with Segun anymore.

On this particular night, Segun had decided to use the charm the fetish priest gave him. Of course, Segun strongly suspected the man seducing his wife was Chief Lamidi Sokoya. Who else could it be? Doja had been teaching his children extra lessons. But how could anyone ever think anything could happen with Lamidi's wife being around most of the time. Moreover, he had tried unsuccessfully, to stop her from continuing the lesson. He could hardly control Doja. She provided the money for food.

Consequently, her usual response was, "we need the extra money from the lessons if we are to eat." Since Segun had no stable job, he was almost always forced into silence. Alas, he could no longer bear it. It was apparent she was having an affair and he must do something.

Recently the news broke out that Chief Sokoya had broken up his thirteen-year old marriage with Abike. It was the talk of the village. It was unbelievable. For some months before the break-up, Lamidi could no longer see anything good in Abike. He found fault with almost everything she did. Abike did everything she knew to correct the situation but to no avail. She could not even complain when Lamidi went out of the house for hours on end and returned late in the night without offering any explanation. Neither would Lamidi eat her food any longer.

Abike was simply confused. She could not place her finger on the root of the problem, though she perceived it must be another woman. 'But who is the woman for heaven's sake?' she racked her brain. Because of her trust and love for Doja, and the wonderful work she was doing on her children, it hardly crossed her mind that she could be connected with her marital woes. It was apparent that Lamidi had changed. He no longer loved her. It was therefore not a surprise to her when Lamidi woke up one morning and commanded her to pack up and get out of his house and return to her parents. Abike pleaded for hours on end to no avail. She invited some respected neighbours to beg Lamidi, but Lamidi was adamant. Thus, was Abike forcefully ejected from her matrimonial home. It was a sorrowful day for Tola and Bisi. They wept and wept until they went off to sleep without eating.

Meanwhile at the Akinyemi's house, Segun slept on the sofa whilst waiting for Doja. It was twelve minutes to eleven at night when Segun woke up with a start. He jumped up to check the time. The key was still in the key hole. Doja had not returned again. Though she had told him she would be seeing her mother that day, but he knew better. It's always one thing or another. Segun was infuriated and jealous. "This is the last time this will happen," Segun swore under his breath. He walked to the door to ensure the black thread the fetish priest gave him was still in place. The instruction from the priest was that he should spread it across a path he was sure his wife would take. Once she crosses the black thread, a spell would be cast on her. Any man, apart from the husband, who made love to her thereafter would crow like a cock three times and die instantly. "Yes, Doja can't escape it this time around. She and her lover shall be exposed and disgraced," Segun reassured himself.

Just then, he heard someone trying the door but noticing there was a key in the lock, the person began to bang at the door. "Open up, Segun, why did you lock me out?" Doja's high pitched voice rang through the night. Reluctantly and without speaking, Segun walked to the door to open it. He pulled the door in and with a feigned smile, welcomed Doja. In anger and without looking in his direction, she hissed and walked to her room. Doja had crossed the black thread without realizing it. With the sound of Doja's bedroom door slamming shut, Segun quickly retrieved the black thread and went to hide it. "It is done," he muttered with satisfaction. "The cat would soon be let out of the bag." However, he thought it would be right to warn her for the last time, especially now that the spell is on her.

"Doja, please let me see you before you sleep. There is something important we must discuss," Segun pleaded.

With a reluctant tone Doja responded without opening the door, "Oh, what is it again. I am tired, I want to sleep."

Segun persisted, "Please, it is important."

Reluctantly, Doja came out frowning. Despite the frown, Segun could not help desiring his wife. Doja was looking sexy and appealing in her night grown. Segun almost forgot the reason for calling her. He made an attempt to touch her.

"Don't touch me," Doja snapped whilst drawing back repulsively. "If you don't speak up now, I'll get back to bed!"

Disappointed and angry at the same time, Segun withdrew his hand, and for the first time, literally shouted at Doja. "Do you treat me like a dog? Well, I have warned you enough. If truly you are having an affair with another man, you would soon be exposed. But I want to strongly advise you to stop such an affair now to avoid disgrace and sorrow."

Doja laughed sarcastically. She had heard it so many times. 'What can he do?' She thought. "Now, Mr. Akinyemi, is that the reason why you called me? Thank you, Mr. Adviser, if you don't have any other serious matter to discuss, please excuse me." She turned briskly and walked off wriggling her waist seductively.

Segun shook his head in dismay and returned to his room thinking, "She will soon discover that I can do a lot."

Bisi balanced a bucket of water on her head while carrying a bowl with both hands. She walked delicately from the back of the house towards the kitchen. She was trying to save time. There were so many things to do all at once. Since Abike her mother had left, the burden of housekeeping and cooking had wholly shifted on her. It was quite a task. She hardly had time for her schoolwork. Thank God it was holiday time now. She was about to drop the bucket of water when a lizard sped past her leg touching her briefly. She screamed and jumped thus throwing off the bucket of water. The loud noise of the iron bucket on wooden structures and splashing water filled the air. Lamidi heard it and rushed to her aid.

"What happened? Sorry," Lamidi empathized while pulling her from the floor. He picked a dry cloth and dried the water on her body. He felt sorry for her. He knew the work was getting too much for her. He had just conceived a plan to send the children to their mum for a holiday. That way, Bisi would be relieved while he would have time to sort out himself. Moreover, he would have more time for Doja. His heart beat faster at the thought of Doja. Over the last few months, he had grown in love with Doja so much that he was becoming convinced nothing could separate them any longer. He was to meet Doja that evening. He would tell her about his plan.

The following day, Lamidi called his children, "Bisi, Tola, you are now on holiday. It is good you spend part of the holiday with your mother, so go and start putting your things together."

Bisi and Tola were happy. They had missed their mother so much. With excitement they began to put their clothes together. Within minutes, they were ready.

Lamidi led them to the village lorry park. They waited for almost three hours before the lorry was filled with passengers. The lorry eventually took off around 3 p.m.

Lamidi returned to the house thinking about Doja. He had barely entered when he heard a knock on the door. He knew instantly it was Doja. She had a habit of knocking three consecutive times before pausing. He rushed to the door to open it. He was right. Standing in front of the door with her usual bewitching smile was Doja. She was looking exceptionally beautiful in a short fluffy black blouse. Doja never once looked like a villager. That was part of the reason for Lamidi's attraction to her. With a wide smile, he beckoned her to come inside.

Doja had barely entered when he banged the door and grabbed her for a hug.

Doja tried pushing him away as she whispered, "The children, do you want them to see us?" Lamidi silenced her with a kiss before pausing to answer her. "They are not in; they have gone on holiday with their mum."

Doja relaxed and melted into Lamidi's arms. They continued fondling, kissing, caressing, and saying a lot of sweet-nonsense as they found their way into the bedroom.

They had barely started making love when Lamidi suddenly stiffened like someone suffering an attack of epilepsy. His eyeballs dilated in agony and pain. He began to crow like a cock. Doja was paralyzed with fear. "Lamidi, Lamidi, Lamidi …" She shouted while frantically shaking him so he could regain his consciousness. It was too late to help Lamidi. Within minutes, Lamidi had died of 'Magun.' It was the effect of the charmed black thread Doja unknowingly crossed the night she returned home late.

Realizing what had happened, Doja quickly dressed up and ran out of the house, calling for help. Within minutes, Chief Lamidi's house was besieged with almost all the inhabitants of Yawiri. Doja was screaming and shaking like a leaf. She could almost not believe what had happened. It was like a bad dream. She immediately knew it was Segun who had done it. She could remember his last words of warning. In-between sobs; she kept mumbling, "Segun, you have killed me …"

Some elderly men moved into the house and quickly performed some rituals before packing Lamidi's body. Some of the women had to pull Doja away as she attempted to follow the men carrying Lamidi's corpse. She became hysterical. With the help of some men, they managed to take her back to her house. Many of the onlookers were shaking their heads in amazement. The question on their lips was, "How could you do this, shameless woman?"

Segun has heard the news and had remained in-doors. "At last, the cat is out of the bag," he mused. He was pacing up and down when Doja was brought to the house. He barricaded the door and with a fierce look commanded that she should not be brought to his house. He rushed in and began to fling out Doja's properties. Segun could not be stopped. He kept repeating, "I have warned her."

It was Bola, an old friend of Doja, that eventually saved her the shame and humiliation, at least temporarily. Doja was thus forced to put up with Bola. However, she could hardly venture out of the house. The scorn and jeers from the villagers would not allow her. At a point in time, Bola had to advise her to leave Yawiri, having heard from reliable source that some youths were planning to lynch her.

"Is this really happening to me or am I having a bad dream?" She kept asking herself. With tears streaming down her face, Doja packed her load. By nightfall of the third day after the sordid episode, Doja ran out of Yawiri.

The news had reached Abike. She wept and wept and could not be pacified. What pained her more was the information that the person in whom she had so much trust and confidence, was the very person responsible for all her woes. She took up a lamentation.

'The world is tough!
How else can you explain it?
A trusted friend
Someone you treated like your own sister Is the same person who
stabs you at the back
The world is tough!'

She had a tough time pacifying Bisi and Tola, particularly Bisi. She had grown very fond of her father. Abike, Tola and Bisi mourned for Lamidi for many days after his death.

CHAPTER 12 HIRED AS HOUSE HELP

The dust had settled. The mysterious death of Chief Lamidi Sokoya was no longer the talk of the village. It had become water that had passed under the bridge. Chief Lamidi virtually left nothing for his family, except perhaps for the mud-house they were living in. Abike refused to return to Yawiri. The memory was too gruesome for her to bear. She decided to live in her parents' village, Langbodo. Langbodo however was not too far from Yawiri.

School had resumed. Bisi was desperate to resume schooling. She had missed one year of schooling already. Abike could only pay Tola's school fee. She desperately wanted Bisi to continue schooling but alas, after spending hours cutting and selling firewood and some of her farm products, she simply could not afford it. Life was tough and unbearable shouldering two person's responsibilities. In desperation, and more because of Bisi's continual pestering, she had to consult some of her friends and relatives for help. No one was ready to help. She was almost giving up when one evening her old-time friend Mama Sikira visited her. In the course of the visit, she informed her about the Manager of Odo-Oba Community Bank who needed a house-help. It was thus arranged that Bisi should be taken to see the Manager very early the following day.

The time was fifteen minutes to seven in the morning when Mama Sikira, Abike and Bisi got to the house of Mr. Silas Sumonu, the Manager of Odo-Oba Community Bank. It was a big bungalow. The visitors knocked repeatedly until their knuckles began to ache.

They were almost giving up when a handsome middle-aged man peeped from one of the windows and asked, "Who are you looking for?" After they had explained their mission, he opened the door and ushered them into the living room. "Who told you I need a house-help?" Mr. Sunmonu further interrogated.

Mama Sikira responded, "It was your security man in the bank. He is the senior brother of my husband's friend?"

Mr. Sunmonu inspected Bisi with interest. She is a pretty young girl. She looks smart and intelligent. "I only hope she can work hard?" he thought. Then he asked for her name and age. "Her name is Bisi, she will be twelve years in two-month's-time," Abike answered.

"She looks so young. Are you sure she can work hard? I want her to go to school. Combining school-work with household work is not an easy job," Mr. Sunmonu explained.

Abike and Bisi impulsively leaped with joy when Mr. Sunmonu said he wanted Bisi to attend school.

Between rolling on the floor and kneeling to thank Mr. Sunmonu for the unexpected miracle, Abike desperately re-assured him, "Sir, she has been prepared for this kind of work. Since she started schooling, she has been combining her schoolwork with household chores. She is not a lazy girl at all."

Still on her knees, Abike requested Mama Sikira to thank Mr. Sunmonu for his benevolence.

Stand up mama, Silas told Abike. "It is okay. I will try her for three months in the first instance, if I am satisfied with her conduct, she will continue, else I will have to send her back to you. For this reason, I will only pay the school fees for one term in the first instance. In addition, I'll give her a monthly allowance of 1000 naira per month. Is that okay?"

"Thank you, Sir," Abike, Mama Sikira and Bisi again knelt to express appreciation to Mr. Sunmonu.

"When can she start work?" Silas inquired.

"She is ready to start straight away Sir. We brought her clothes and things. She can start now," Abike responded with excitement.

She could hardly believe what was happening. 'I must warn Bisi to be careful to not waste this golden opportunity,' she thought.

Abike drew Bisi close to her side. "Bisi, be a good girl. Remember how we suffered this past one year trying to get you back to school. And here you have a golden opportunity to return to school. Serve your master well."

The death of Lamidi had thrown mother and daughter into a much closer relationship. They had drawn much warmth and comfort from each other. That was what made the parting such a traumatic event for Bisi. She could not hold back her tears at the thought of leaving her mother. Abike too felt a lump in her throat. She was doing her best to suppress her emotions. They both knew that if Bisi must continue her education and ultimately help the family, the parting was inevitable.

In between sobs, Bisi reassured her mum, "Mama, I will not disappoint you. You know I am not a lazy girl. And thank you Mama Sikira." She knelt to thank Mama Sikira.

Mr. Sunmonu was touched. Instinctively, he knew there wouldn't be any need to send away this girl. At that moment, a car screeched to a halt outside the house. A man entered and greeted Mr. Sunmonu and the visitors. It was Joseph, Mr. Sunmonu's driver.

Facing his visitors, Mr. Sunmonu said, "Now I must go to work. Let Bisi use the day to settle down. Tomorrow, I will send my driver to take her to school. She should be able to continue her school by tomorrow. You can also come and check her anytime you want. I will also allow her to spend one weekend in a month with you."

Mr. Sunmonu gave Abike and Mama Sikira 50 naira each for their transport. Abike, Mama Sikira and Bisi again knelt to express their gratitude. Thereafter, Abike and Mama Sikira returned to Langbodo and Yawiri respectively.

Thus, Bisi commenced work as a house help. Though Mr. Silas had not told her what to do, using her initiative, she swept the house, washed plates and washed the dirty clothes piled up in a corner.

She finally settled down to revise schoolwork. She had barely read for five minutes when she dozed off. It was the sound of the revving car that woke her up around 6pm. Mr. Sunmonu had returned from work.

CHAPTER 13 THE TERRIBLE TRIAL

Six years had rolled by since Bisi took on the job of house-help. Luckily, a secondary school opened at Odo-oba where she lived. She took the common entrance exam whilst in Primary 5 and emerged the best candidate. She no longer had to walk about five kilometers each day, as she used to when attending school at Yawiri. Bisi was already in secondary school class four.

Everything seemed to be going well for Bisi. She had been selected as the Senior Female Prefect when the school started. She maintained this post all through her secondary school days. Thus, Bisi successfully reached the final year class. Bisi was hardworking at home and at school. Mr Sunmonu hardly had cause to find fault in her work in all the six years.

Despite the countless household chores, she had to run, Bisi coped well. She was always cheerful, even in the face of mounting work pressure. Never once did she complain. Neither would she use the excuse to neglect her schoolwork. She was a self-motivated, disciplined girl. When faced with the opportunity to choose between watching television and studying, Bisi often chose reading, studying and doing her school assignments. She at times asked Mr. Sunmonu to explain some difficult concepts. Consequently, her results had always been good.

As the years rolled by, Bisi grew from being a young immature girl into a lovely young lady. Tall, slim with a smooth fair skin, she became the cynosure of all the young men in the village. She was like a lovely flower in the garden to which all the butterflies were drawn. Even some lecherous old men could not keep their eyes off Bisi. But with all these, Bisi never once lost her sense of balance and discipline. She stayed focused on her schooling. She had no time for the frivolities girls of her age engaged in. In time, even Mr. Sunmonu began to struggle with his emotion over Bisi. The girl's emerging beauty was not lost on him either. It was not long before he started to feel a twinge of jealousy and over-protectiveness whenever he noticed anybody, especially males giving Bisi admiring glances or compliments. Mr. Sunmonu had a hard time keeping within the boundary of merely admiring Bisi.

Instinctively, Bisi began to sense subtle changes in her master's attitude towards her. In his tone of voice, his quick furtive looks and general body language, Bisi thought she sensed something deeper than just likeness. Perhaps she was just imagining things. But she kept all these thoughts to herself.

Bisi could hardly forget the events that led to her father's mysterious death. It was after the sad event that she was able to put the jigsaw puzzles together. The experience had made her to resolutely decide that she would never conduct herself like Aunty Doja. "I will not allow any man to mess up my life, neither will I mess up other people's lives or marriages like Aunty Doja did."

Alas, Bisi's suspicions about Mr. Sunmonu was getting confirmed with each passing moment. His expression of affection was no longer hidden. The gifts were becoming more frequent and more expensive. Initially, she counted it to be a mere show of appreciation for her hard work. But in recent times, he had gotten bolder in telling her affectionate words like, "Bisi, you are so pretty. You know I love you. Feel free with me, will you?"

Bisi was getting confused. Her greatest fear however was displeasing Mr. Sunmonu, especially now that she was so close to taking her final Secondary School Certificate Examination.

Bisi had just returned from school. The school principal had informed them that the deadline for registering for the school certificate examination was two weeks' time. She was desperate. Mr. Sunmonu had refused to give her the money. He would only release the money on the condition that Bisi went to bed with him. Bisi had been resisting steadfastly. "I would rather not do the exam than go to bed with Mr. Sunmonu," she muttered repeatedly to herself.

Mr. Sunmonu on his part was getting more desperate by the day. Just before leaving the office that day, he made up his mind to send Bisi away that night if she still refused to cooperate. Not able to control himself any longer, he closed from work early. He knew Bisi would be at home already.

Bisi was reading on the dining table when Mr. Sunmonu got home. As usual, she greeted him kneeling whilst she collected his briefcase to take to his bedroom. Mr. Sunmonu was expecting that. So, he followed her closely and locked the bedroom door.

Bisi was instantly alarmed. 'What next? I must fight for my life,' she frantically thought. Her eyes and mind darted around searching for a way of escape. She suddenly conceived an idea. As she had suspected, Mr. Sunmonu approached her with a seductive smile while drawing Bisi close for an embrace.

He was surprised at Bisi's reaction. He was expecting a hot resistance as usual. He was about to start fondling Bisi's breasts when she gently held his hand and with a patronizing tone, she said, "Mr. Sunmonu, I have thought about your proposals. I am ready to cooperate. Can you please allow me to wash myself? I have not done so since I returned from school. I will be back in a moment."

Mr. Sunmonu fell for it. It was the first time he had a positive response from Bisi. So, without much ado, he released her and opened the bedroom door.

"It worked!" Bisi muttered with excitement as she calmly walked out of the room. Once out, she dashed into her room and locked the door. 'What will I do next?' She frantically reasoned.

She was still desperately thinking of the next thing to do when Mr. Sunmonu came banging on the door. He realized he had been fooled. Like a wounded lion, he banged hard on the door with his fist. Bisi was terrified. She began to pray.

"Look, I give you thirty minutes to pack your load. You are

leaving this house tonight, and I mean tonight. I don't want to see you in this house anymore. I can no longer sponsor your education either. Imagine a small girl like you making a fool of me." Still fuming, he left off banging Bisi's door and returned to his bedroom.

Bisi realized it would be dangerous to continue to stay in the house. With tears streaming down her face, she frantically packed her few belongings. Her greatest sorrow was that this event had happened at a most crucial moment in her life when she desperately needed peace of mind and financial support to be able to do her final Secondary School Examination. Important as this desire was, she resolutely made up her mind she would not yield to Mr. Sunmonu's illicit advances. The memory of Aunty Doja and her father was too fresh in her mind for her to be lured into the same trap. "Yes, I must leave Mr. Sunmonu's house tonight."

Sensing that Mr. Sunmonu was no longer outside the door, Bisi quietly opened the door and tip-toed her way into the living room. She was almost getting to the main door when Mr. Sunmonu came charging from his bedroom. Because the door of the living room was almost facing Mr. Sunmonu's bedroom door, he instantly spotted Bisi.

Silas Sunmonu was in full rage. "After all I have done for you, you have to treat me this way?" he shouted.

Frantic, Bisi tried unsuccessfully to open the door's lock. Out of fear she kept missing the turn that would open the door. Mr. Sunmonu, roaring with anger, was getting closer. Bisi was in literal terror. With shaking hands, she eventually succeeded in opening the door and ran out just before Mr. Sunmonu could reach her. She was however not spared of verbal assaults. Full of sorrow, and with tears streaming her face while sobbing silently, Bisi left Mr. Sunmonu's house and walked into the dark night not knowing where to go.

Eventually, Bisi slept in one of her school-mate's houses that night. She left Odo-Oba for Langbodo the following day. Abike could hardly believe the story.

"When did it start?" She inquired.

"I don't really know, but I only started noticing it when he began to give me lots of gifts. And then he started to tell me how much he liked me. I thought it was all a joke because I had always seen him as my father."

Abike began to cry, "But why now? How are you going to complete your school now? With only few months to go. This must be the work of the devil."

After some minutes of crying, Abike conceived an idea. She wiped her face and shared the idea with Bisi. "Bisi, you know I don't have any means of helping you now. Your brother Tola had to stop schooling because I could no longer pay his school fees. He is now farming to raise some money. We hope we will be able to raise enough money by next year so he can resume his schooling. But your case is an emergency one. This is your final exam. Why don't you go and meet your uncle in Lagos? Perhaps he will be able to help you. He has just returned from London."

The idea appealed to Bisi. It is true. Uncle Timothy should be able to help. With excitement and a ray of hope, she decided to travel to Lagos the following day.

CHAPTER 14 THE BROKEN DAM EXPERIENCE

Bisi managed to complete her secondary school education and secured admission into University of Ibadan through the help of Uncle Timothy. She was admitted to study Electrical Engineering.

Alas, she was about to complete the second semester of her second session when she received the shocking news that Uncle Timothy had died in a ghastly motor accident. Bisi wept for days and could hardly be consoled. The sad event affected her so much that she fell sick and had to briefly go home for better care. Bisi returned to campus two weeks later totally demoralized.

Uncle Timothy had been her only source of financial help. Even with his help, it was not easy for Bisi to make ends meet. What uncle Timothy had been giving her was barely enough to pay her school fees and purchase some books and materials.

There was also the brewing temptation to have a love affair, which has been growing stronger by the day. She kept wondering how long she would be able to keep the boys and men away. Campus life was a different experience altogether. The flashy dresses of some of the girls, the flashy cars and the general flashy mode of life were too much for Bisi to ignore. She occasionally wondered how she had been able to endure temptations so far. The financial challenge was further magnifying the temptation.

One particular boy named Tunde was persistent. Tunde, also a student of faculty of engineering, had a car and had been generous to her. Of-course, Bisi knew the time was getting close for her to marry. She knew it was about time to start looking out for Mr. Right. She was however resolute to complete her university education before embarking on such an exercise. "I don't want distractions now," she kept saying.

Since the death of Uncle Timothy, Bisi has been doing some serious thinking. She kept reassuring herself, "Nothing will stop me from completing my university education, not even the death of Uncle Timothy. But what will I do now? Who can I turn to for help?"

The more she tried to brush away the thought of Tunde, the rich young agricultural engineering student, the more she found her mind coming back to him.

In retrospect, Bisi mused, "Tunde seems to be the only solution to my predicament. Of course, I like him. He is handsome, rich, intelligent and well-behaved. And more importantly, he is not a married person. The only thing I don't know too well about him is whether he has other girlfriends or not."

Bisi was still thinking about Tunde and how he could be the solution to her current financial challenge when she heard a knock on the door. She was the only one in the room. Her roommates had all gone out. "Hold on," she responded. she adjusted her dress, touched up a little in front of the mirror and went to open the door. She was pleasantly surprised to find Tunde at the door. With his usual captivating smile, he stretched out his hand to shake her hand. Bisi offered Tunde a seat.

"Could this be a coincidence or God's way of telling me I am right?" Bisi thought. Tunde's voice brought her back to reality.

"Bisi, I learnt you fell ill. I was informed your uncle died in a motor accident. Please accept my condolence. I have checked on you several times in the past two weeks but was told you weren't back. Nobody knew exactly when you'd be back, so I had to keep trying. Guess I am lucky to meet you tonight."

Bisi felt so loved and cared for. The thought coupled with the remembrance of the loss of her uncle suddenly stirred her emotions. Almost uncontrollably, she began to sob.

Tunde was confused. "Have I said anything wrong?" he inquired.

Bisi shook her   head   while   still sobbing.

Almost without thinking, he sprang to her side on the bed,

drew her close and with his left hand around her shoulders he gently mopped the tears running down her pretty face with a white handkerchief. "Oh, Bisi, please don't cry anymore. It's alright. Please don't cry."

It was the first time they had been this close. Tunde found himself loving Bisi more than ever before. Of course, he had other girlfriends, yet none of them seemed to compare with Bisi. "Bisi is so disciplined. She is not cheap like the other girls," Tunde thought as he continued to pacify her.

Gradually Bisi regained her composure. Tunde's arm was still around her shoulder. Gradually, another emotion seemed to take over. Tunde was the first to perceive it. Rather than take his arm away, he found himself holding her hands while looking deep into her eyes. Bisi could not resist the emotion, not with Tunde's touch. The thought of removing her hands or drawing away from him never crossed her mind. It seemed so natural they should be like that. She felt a strange wave of love emotion overwhelming her.

Tunde's head was drawing closer to hers. Almost unconsciously, she closed her eyes as Tunde's lips touched hers. The lip contact created an explosive feeling in Bisi's head. She had never experienced anything like this before. Of course, it was her first time of kissing a man.

Momentarily, the wall of her resistance came tumbling down. She found herself drawn along the wave of passionate feelings. In spite of herself, she submitted to the warm, loving feeling coursing through her whole being. Tunde, who was more experienced, began to caress her. At this point, Bisi felt like a broken dam, with the strong waves of bursting water sweeping off every ounce of resistance on its path. She had lost total control of the strong waves of love emotion that had suddenly swept over her. Tunde somehow sensed he could easily make love to her at this point. He actually began to make moves to this end. He had managed to push Bisi onto the bed when a knock on the door broke the spell and instantly brought them back to their senses. Bisi quickly jumped up, adjusted her dress while beckoning to Tunde to move back to the chair.

"Hold on, I'm coming," she managed to respond calmly as the knocking persisted. Finally, she opened the door. It was the younger sister of Sandra, one of Bisi's roommates. She had brought a message from Sandra's parents. Bisi welcomed her warmly and explained that Sandra had been out since morning. She then encouraged her to leave the message, assuring her that she would deliver it.

By this time Bisi had regained her composure. She knew she had gone too far with Tunde. "Yes, I'm interested in him, but I shouldn't sell myself so cheap."

Tunde felt he had missed a golden opportunity. All effort to resume the love exchange were met with resistance from Bisi. Eventually, Bisi stood up and advised him to leave as her roommates are likely to return anytime.

"Bisi, it's all right. I'll leave. But tell me something. You know I love you so much, don't you love me too?"

Bisi refused to answer though her whole body was crying, "I love you Tunde," but somehow, she managed to hold her tongue. "I must be careful not to sell myself cheap to this rich young man who thinks he can have whatever and whoever he wants."

But Tunde was persistent. "Bisi, I need an answer to this one important question. I love you so much. Will you marry me?"

Bisi was dazed. The death of Uncle Timothy made her so vulnerable. Bisi felt it would be wise to commit herself to a relationship with Tunde now. She definitely needed him. With an air of reluctance and hesitation, Bisi responded, "I love you too Tunde, but please give me time to think about it." Tunde was excited. From experience, he knew what that meant.

He rushed towards Bisi to hug and kiss her. Realizing the danger of allowing him to kiss her again, she restrained him.

"Not again tonight, you can leave now please." Bisi opened the door for Tunde.

Somehow, he couldn't understand this girl called Bisi. Only few minutes ago, he was at the verge of making love to her, but now it was as if the episode never happened. The paradoxical reactions made her more exciting and fascinating to Tunde. Reluctantly, Tunde left, happy that she had at least not outrightly rejected his proposal for marriage.

CHAPTER 15 VIRGIN AT 22?

Bisi had finally agreed to marry Tunde after their graduation. The relationship between Bisi and Tunde had grown deeper in the past two years. Over the months, they had kissed and caressed, but somehow Bisi had been able to prevent the 'broken dam' experience recurring. At times she was amazed at how she had been able to cope, especially with a passionate young man like Tunde. Somehow, she knew she had gained Tunde's respect and love more because she had not sold herself cheap.

Tunde's parents did not approve of the relationship. They preferred Tunde's former fiancée, Tina, the daughter of a chief justice. They couldn't bring themselves to accept Bisi whom they saw as a pauper and an opportunist who had only succeeded in bewitching and feeding fat on their son.

Tunde had repeatedly assured Bisi not to be disturbed by his parent's attitude. "With time, as they get to know you better, I know they will change their mind."

Tunde's respect for Bisi was further shown in the way he carefully covered up concerning his other girlfriends. He rather preferred the other girls to know about Bisi being his fiancée than for Bisi to know about them. The respect and love, however, could be questioned because Tunde still took his other girlfriends to bed whilst giving Bisi the impression she was his only partner.

Tunde worked hard to prove his love for Bisi. The experience of each passing day seemed to convince her of the seriousness of Tunde and the sincerity of his affection for her. She knew that she might not be able to hold back Tunde much longer.

A few weeks after, she attended a wedding ceremony of one of Tunde's senior sisters. The wedding was held at Tunde's hometown in Ilorin. Ilorin is about three hours journey from Ibadan. The ceremony ended late so they could not return to Ibadan that same day. Thus, was Bisi forced to sleep in the same room with Tunde, for lack of space. There was just one bed in the room. Bisi feared that what she had dreaded for so long was about to come to pass. She could not fathom how she would escape Tunde's advances this time around, alone, in the same bed, all night long. Furthermore, because they had to preserve their clothes from getting wrinkled, they were forced to remove them and use the bedding as wrapper.

In order to change, Bisi took permission from Tunde to put off the light. Smiling to himself, he consented. Feeling awkward in the dark, Bisi took off her skirt and blouse and wrapped herself with one of the bedsheets. She switched on the light and slipped into bed facing the wall. She avoided looking at Tunde who had removed the top of his clothing thus baring his hairy muscular chest and biceps.

"I know how to catch her," Tunde smiled wryly. "Bisi, is this for you?" he asked waving his finger in the air.

Bisi fell for his trick instinctively. She turned to look at him. Tunde laughed. She discovered only too late that he was playing games. For the first time, Bisi had a good view of Tunde's masculine features. Her heartbeat suddenly skipped. Her emotions rose almost uncontrollably. She quickly turned her eyes away again. Tunde knew he had got her. Calmly he switched off the light and got into bed.

Gently but firmly, Tunde began to caress her back while whispering words of love into her ears. Bisi tried to draw away from his caress. Albeit, the bed was too small for her to pull away. Thus, she resigned herself to fate.

"Bisi, won't you kiss me goodnight." Of course, they'd been kissing. So Bisi knew she couldn't refuse. Reluctantly, she turned to kiss Tunde; but tonight was different. They were both virtually naked. There was more skin contact. Bisi's self-control was fast ebbing out. Then it happened. The broken dam experience she had the first time she kissed Tunde in the dormitory occurred again. Bisi lost self-control. Almost unconsciously, she abandoned herself. It was not until she felt the sharp pain of her virginity being broken, she realized what was happening. Tunde had succeeded at last in plucking the flower she had been keeping for the past twenty-two years. Somehow, she did not regret it. He had been so nice to her. She wouldn't have completed her education without his support.

Tunde was pleasantly surprised. He was surprised that it was still possible to find a virgin in the university and in the final year. His respect for Bisi grew. After cleaning up, he hugged her closely and kept reassuring her with words of love. So, they slept in each other's arms.

The sun was already streaming into the room when Bisi opened her eyes. Almost in frenzy, she woke up Tunde. They got dressed and travelled back to Ibadan

CHAPTER 16 THE AIDS SAGA

The examination timetable was out. It was the end of the session semester examination. Students were busy reading, studying and researching for facts and information relevant to their courses. Students were naturally sober at this period. Tunde was heading towards the university library. He felt so weak and tired. He had been suffering different kinds of sickness for many months now. Initially it was bouts of Malaria. Not long after, he began stooling. That went on for almost six months. Hardly would food stay in his stomach. He didn't feel like eating most of the time. Consequently, he had become terribly emaciated. Mustering every ounce of energy left in him, as he began to climb the library staircase, the sick feeling surfaced again. He had barely finished climbing the staircase when he began to throw up. It was the eighth time he had vomited that day. He had been defecating too. The sickness seemed to be getting worse. It was as if his bowels would come out any minute. Almost unexpectedly, Tunde lost consciousness. Concerned students and library officials ran to his aid. When the attempts to revive him proved abortive, they rushed him to the university clinic.

Tunde was still unconscious when his blood sample was taken for laboratory test. Finally, the result came out. Tunde was HIV positive. He had reached an advanced stage of AIDS. He was thus kept on drip mixed with some palliative drugs.

Eventually, he regained consciousness. Groaning slightly, his eyes darted around trying to decipher where he was. The nurses came to his bedside. They had searched his pocket for clues on any of his relatives or friends they could contact.

One of the nurses offered him an explanation. "You fainted on your way to the library. That was why you were brought here. This is the university clinic."

Another nurse asked, "what is your name?"

"Tunde. Tunde Babatope."

The nurse left and soon returned with Tunde's hospital card. She wrote something on the card and then asked, "Who is your next of kin? Someone who can take care of you while you are in the clinic."

Without hesitation, he responded, "Bisi, Bisi Sokoya. She is a final year student in the department of Electrical Engineering."

The nurse wrote the information on a piece of paper and gave it to a male nurse attendant with an instruction to invite Bisi to the clinic. Bisi was in the hostel studying when she got the news about Tunde. Somehow, she was not surprised. She had been disturbed about Tunde's health for some time now. She frantically got dressed, picked up some of her provisions and rushed to the clinic.

Tunde was still awake when she got there. The medical doctor on duty was on ward round. Not minding the nurses around, Bisi rushed towards Tunde and tenderly held him looking intently into his face.

Emaciated Tunde on hospital bed, with Bisi by the bedside
"How are you feeling, my love? What do they say is wrong?"

"I don't know," Tunde weakly mumbled.

Not long after, the doctor and his team got to Tunde. Peering at Bisi above a pair of round-eyed glasses that were perched almost at the tip of his nose, the doctor asked, "Are you his next of kin?"

"Yes, I am his fiancée," Bisi responded.

"Well then, I'll like to talk to both of you in my office."

"Nurse, please conduct the patient in a wheelchair to my office."

Within minutes, they were all seated. With a serious look on his face, the doctor cleared his throat while inspecting the medical report. After what seemed like a long silence, he said pointedly:

"Tunde has been diagnosed with HIV/AIDS. The disease has reached an advanced stage. As you know..." Bisi felt a cold chill ran down her spine. She screamed and fainted. The doctor, with the assistance of the nurse, worked frantically to revive her.

By the time she regained her full consciousness, she was lying on a bed. She recollected what the doctor had said. The implication and enormity of the report dawned on her. Virtually all students are aware of the terrible disease called AIDS. They are aware of the consequences of AIDS. The awareness programme on AIDS had been so intense on campus. Never once did Bisi conceive the thought that her beloved Tunde could be infected.

"Why God, why are you taking someone who is so dear to my heart again?" She began to sob. The nurses could hardly pacify her. The news was too devastating. She was still sobbing and reflecting on the news when the memory of the night they had together at Ilorin came back to her.

"Oh no," She silently prayed. "Oh God, let it not be that I have contacted the disease too. Oh God, please?" She could no longer lie down. She desperately wanted to be sure. She jumped off the bed and asked for the doctor.

"Please, nurse, take me to the doctor. There is something very important I must tell him. It is urgent"

The nurse yielded and took Bisi to the doctor. "Yes, can I help you lady? Please sit down." Bisi sat down anxiously wringing her hands. The nurse left the room.

"Doctor, I want to tell you that I made love with Tunde not too long ago. Could I have got the disease also? Please I want to know," Bisi pleaded as she broke down in tears. The doctor picked up a tissue paper and gave it to Bisi to dry up her tears.

"Please don't cry. Let's conduct the test first. It is possible you have not contacted it."

Tunde was moved to the male ward. He was still asleep. Bisi sat beside his bed. As memories of their good times flooded through her mind, she began to sob. A nurse walked up to Tunde's bed to inform Bisi that the doctor would like to see her. Her heartbeat raced. With shaky legs, she walked up to the consulting room. This time around, the doctor did not allow the nurse to leave. He was in a pensive mood. Bisi could sense bad news coming. She could no longer wait.

"Doctor, what is it. What is the result?"

"Please be calm. After another brief period of silence, he finally spoke up, "I am sorry to tell you that you are also HIV positive."

Bisi broke out in cold sweat, "Oh no, it can't be. It was only once. And it was the only time in my life I ever met a man. Oh no, how can life be so cruel?"

The doctor had to give her a sedative. Almost against her will, she fell asleep. Not too long after, she was running. No one was chasing her. The road appeared plain before her. The breeze was exhilarating. She was enjoying the race. She continued running with abandon. Almost abruptly, she began to fall. It was as if the ground has suddenly opened up into a bottomless pit. Down and down the big black hole she went. Bisi screamed, "Somebody help me... help me, please help me."

These were the words on her lips as the nurse on duty repeatedly shook her to wake her. Her heartbeat was still racing when she woke up. She realized she had been dreaming.

Soon after awaking, she recollected the medical reports. She sighed repeatedly. She felt like committing suicide. "How I wish the whole issue was a bad dream like the one I just had," she mused. But alas, it was real. Still reflecting, she mumbled, "Tunde will soon die of AIDS, and very soon it will be my turn." With an air of resignation, she moaned, "Oh God, what will I do now?"

Almost impulsively, Bisi found her love for Tunde turning to hatred. "Tunde had deceived me. He had other girlfriends all the while. That was how he got the HIV. Yet, he was making me believe I was the only girl in his life. He took advantage of me." Bisi felt bitter as she laid on the hospital bed.

Finally, she summed up courage and made up her mind not to tell anyone about the bad news until after the examination. "I will go straight to my mother after the exams." She resolved. She bade Tunde farewell and promised to inform his parents that he had been admitted.

Bisi managed to complete the final exams. The results came out two weeks after the last paper was taken. She had first class honours in Electrical Engineering. She was the talk of the whole campus. However, rather than being happy, Bisi was sorrowful. Her lecturers and friends could not understand her.

Tunde could not do the exam. He was too weak and feeble to even feed himself. His health deteriorated rapidly. He became totally bedridden.

Bisi was packing her possessions getting ready to return to Langbodo when the sad news of Tunde's death was brought to her. She cried relentlessly. She was sorrowful, not only for Tunde but more for the thought that it would soon be her turn. 'It's a cruel life,' Bisi thought aloud. 'Is this how all my toil and sufferings all these years will end?'

"O, God, if you are truly existing, please save me, I don't want to die yet," Bisi silently prayed with tears streaming down her face.

CHAPTER 17 THE MIRACULOUS DELIVERANCE

It was dark when Bisi reached Langbodo. She did not want anyone to see her. Abike and Tola were eating when she got home. They were both excited and happy to see Bisi. Almost in unison, they asked, "How was the exam? Did you pass?" Bisi nodded in silence.

Gradually, they began to sense something was wrong. Tola collected her baggage while Abike, with arms around her shoulder, led her to a seat. She offered her water. Bisi turned it down. She also refused food.

Sighing deeply, Bisi mumbled, "Mama, I don't feel like eating anything."

Abike could not understand it, "But you passed your exams. Why then are you not happy my child? Tell me, what happened?"

Bisi sighed and kept silent again. Abike could no longer wait, she began to feel apprehensive. "Bisi tell me, what is it? Is it about Tunde your friend?"

Bisi again nodded her head.

"What about him?", Abike asked with agitation.

"Uhmm… Mama, Tunde is dead."

Abike became hysterical. "Tell me it is not true. Bisi tell me it is not true," She echoed relentlessly whilst shaking Bisi.

Tola, who had heard the terrible news gently pulled Abike away from Bisi.

As Tola was drawing her away, she kept asking, "Bisi tell me it is not true. Are we the only people in the world that evil occurrences should keep befalling us?"

Abike and Bisi began to cry. In-between sobs, Bisi continued, "Mama I have not finished. The doctor also said…" she paused. Abike's eyes were dilated in fear. She prodded Bisi, "What did the doctor say?"

"He said I also have the disease that killed Tunde," Bisi

continued in-between sobs.

Abike passed out. Tola quickly went out for a bucket of water whilst Bisi was frantically shaking her mother to revive her.

It took quite a while for Abike to come around. But the shock of the news was still tugging at her heart. She just couldn't comprehend it. "AIDS? It is better I die," she muttered.

"Mama, stop saying that," Tola sternly rebuked her.

Abike was the first to break the deadly silence that followed. "So, what are we going to do now? Didn't they say there is no cure for this disease?"

Bisi nodded in affirmation.

Abike continued, "But I know a herbalist at Abanla. People say he could cure any disease. Let's try him."

Tola was about to protest but quickly held his peace as Abike snapped, "Why are you protesting? Do you have an alternative solution?"

Tola mumbled weakly, "Of-course I don't have a solution. But these juju-men hardly solve problems, they rather add to it."

"You leave that to God. It is better than not trying at all." Facing Bisi, she continued, "Why don't you wash your face, we are going to the herbalist tonight. This is an emergency."

Not long after, Abike, Bisi and Tola were knocking the door of a thatched mud house that was built on the outskirt of Abanla. An elderly white-haired man in tattered clothes opened the door beckoning them to come in. After narrating their challenge, he sighed deeply, paused and cleared his throat.

"It can be done, but it will cost some money."

"Baba, if there is anything we can do to save my daughter's life, please do it. God will provide the money."

The old man stood up and walked out of the hut. He returned a few minutes later carrying some leaves and concoction which he placed before Abike. "This is it. Cook these leaves with plenty of water for three hours. Let her drink and bathe out of it. She must drink the concoction every night before going to bed. And one more thing, I have to make incisions on her head and between her breasts to avert the spirit of death."

Bisi could hardly believe her ears, "Between my breasts?" she asked incredulously.

"Yes, between your breasts and you have to be naked when we are performing the ritual," the old man added with a cold stare.

Bisi began to sob.

Abike pacified her. "Bisi, Akonji ogan [Yoruba eulogy]. Why are you crying? Don't you know it is to save your life? Don't worry about the shame. Nobody is around to see you anyway. Take heart my daughter."

With these words, Bisi stopped sobbing and braced up for the worst. 'I brought it all on myself. If only I had been disciplined enough to keep my virginity until I was married, I wouldn't have been a victim of this ordeal. And all these for a one-time sexual experience,' she whined as her hands broke out in cold sweat. It was around midnight when Abike and her children returned home.

Three days after Bisi commenced using the concoctions prescribed by the herbalist, she developed complications. She almost died of convulsion. What saved her was the new clinic that was opened at Langbodo. Bisi was rushed to the clinic. Though she was revived, yet the medical personnel felt it would be wise to refer her to the teaching hospital at Ibadan. Abike had to go around the village borrowing money to take care of Bisi. They could barely eat even once a day. Life became unbearable for the family.

Bisi was admitted to the intensive care unit of the University of Ibadan teaching hospital for almost six months. The experience threw the widowed family deeper into poverty. There was simply no one to help. When they could no longer cope with the hospital bill, they pleaded for her discharge and promised to be reporting for check-up.

Bisi's condition deteriorated by the day, not so much from the AIDs but because of her emotional turmoil. She became depressive. At one point, she began to contemplate suicide.

"It would at least save my family shame and undue financial stress," she thought.

Yet, another part of her yearned to live. "Oh, how I wish to live and prove to the world that what a man can do a woman can do also, even better," she wailed. "O God please have mercy on me and deliver me from death. I don't want to die yet," Bisi prayed repeatedly. "I promise not to make this terrible mistake again. I also promise to teach youths not to fall into this error."

Torn between the passion to live and the nagging thought of committing suicide, Bisi gradually found herself desiring to read the bible. It was something she had not done for years. The thought kept coming to her that if no one could help her, God could. She recollected vaguely the testimonies some of her friends had been sharing with her on campus about divine healing. 'Perhaps there is something to it after all,' she thought. So, she began to read the bible.

By now Bisi could hardly go outside the house. Almost everyone in the village knew her condition. They avoided her like a leper. It was a terrible experience. It was in moments like this she felt more like committing suicide.

It was a long time since she had taken a stroll. She desired the sunlight and fresh breeze. She had been scared of meeting people. Summoning up courage, she informed Abike she wanted to stroll out with Tola. They had barely stepped out of the house when a crowd suddenly gathered to make a spectacle of her. Tongues were wagging. Some even spoke loud enough for her to hear.

"That's her, the prostitute. She contracted HIV in the university and has now brought it to the village. She should be sent away before she spreads it around the village." They laughed and jeered at her.

Bisi instantly felt sick and weak. Her legs began to wobble, and she would have fallen but for Tola's quick intervention. She managed to mumble, "Tola please take me back to the house. I can't take this anymore. It is better I die."

Bisi began to sob uncontrollably.

Abike heard her wailing even before they entered the house. "What is the problem? What happened?" she inquired.

Tola's explanation was drowned by Bisi's loud cry. Realizing what had happened, Abike began to pacify Bisi. After a long while, Bisi began to calm down. Her eyes were red with tears.

There was a sudden knock on the door.

Tola tried to encourage Bisi and Abike to cheer up for the sake of the visitor but they couldn't care less. The knock came again, stronger this time.

Tola was forced to open the door. He could hardly believe his eyes. He shouted, "Sege! Is this really you or your angel? Please come in, long time no see." They hugged and exchanged more pleasantries.

Tola couldn't have responded otherwise. He saw Segun Obatola ten years earlier after their primary school education. He had left for Lagos to continue his education. They were best friends.

By this time, Bisi had managed to stop crying, though she was still looking very sad. On entering, Segun instantly perceived something was wrong. He prostrated to greet Abike. He stood and greeted Bisi with a handshake.

"What is it? Why are you looking so sad?" Segun inquired facing Tola. Tola was about to answer him when Bisi made a sign for him to keep quiet.

Segun, with his back to Bisi, sensed the reluctance. 'It must be a serious issue,' he sensed. Somehow, Segun could not hold his peace. He knew something was definitely wrong.

"So, what happened, Segun, you look changed," Tola said

admiringly.

"You are correct Tola. When I got to Lagos, I repented and gave my life to Jesus."

"Really?" Tola interjected.

"That was not all. I was also baptized in water and in the Holy Ghost."

Noticing he had been standing since he came in, Abike beckoned him to sit. "My son, please take a seat?"

"Thank you, mama," Segun responded and took a seat.

Eager to know the end of the story, Tola probed further, "So what happened after you were baptized in the Holy Ghost?"

"I joined the hospital and prisons visitation group. In the process, I had opportunity to pray for some patients with terminal diseases like cancer, tumour, diabetes and AIDS. As we ministered to them in the name of Jesus, many of them recovered and were healed."

Bisi, who had not been paying attention to Segun, was all ears when he got to this point. It suddenly dawned on the family that Segun could have an answer to the problem that was causing them sorrow and tears.

"How were they healed?" Bisi interjected!

"The key scriptures we often use to minister to the sick were Isaiah 53: 1-5 and Matthew 8:17. The book of Isaiah says: "Surely, He (i.e. Jesus) hath borne our grieves and carried our sorrows. He was wounded for our transgressions, and by his stripes we were healed. Jesus has paid the price for our sicknesses, pains, sorrows and grieves. Consequently, we are not supposed to suffer sickness and pains again. All it takes is to believe in him."

Bisi was still sceptical.

Abike could not comprehend it too, but somehow, she believed that this young man could help her daughter out of her present predicament.

Bisi asked Segun pointedly, almost with excitement. "Wait Segun, are you saying that if someone is infected with HIV for example, and he believes in Jesus as you have explained, the person shall be healed of the sickness? Is that what you are saying?"

"Bisi, I'm not just saying it, I have seen it confirmed more than once. I was directly involved in one particular case. It was a mysterious case." He dipped his hand into his pocket and brought out two pictures. First, he circulated one picture. In the picture was a skinny emaciated sickly girl of about twenty- two. "That was Sandra at an advanced stage of AIDS. She had only few weeks left to live then, according to the doctors." He circulated another picture, and then continued, "This is the same Sandra. This picture was only taken last month. We are presently in the same activity group in church. The mystery I am referring to is that God recently revealed to me that Sandra is my wife. I have told her, and we are presently engaged."

Bisi, Abike, and Tola could no longer hide their excitement. Still inquisitive, Bisi asked: "How did it happen? I mean how was she healed? What did you do?"

Segun perceived from the trend of discussion that the problem facing this family was not unconnected with AIDS. He therefore took his time to explain.

Finally, he said, "You see, it's so simple. The most important thing is to understand and believe what Jesus has done for us. Thereafter, we lead the person to give his/her life to Christ. Then we pray a simple prayer of faith. We encourage the recipient to believe according to Mark 11:24 that he or she is already healed the moment the prayers are said; that is it. As the person keeps believing, declaring and acting out his or her faith, the healing is manifested."

Almost without realizing what she was doing, Bisi knelt down and pleaded, "Segun, please pray for me, I have been afflicted with HIV." Abike joined her.

"Abba, mama, please stand. Salvation is free. You don't have to beg. Only believe. Let's pray."

They all knelt down as Segun prayed fervently. He led the family to Christ. He further prayed for Bisi to be healed of HIV/AIDS. Thereafter, they sang praises to God. He further assured them it was done. Finally, he challenged Bisi to go for a medical test.

One month later, Bisi and Tola visited Segun, full of joy. God had done it, Bisi was miraculously healed of the deadly HIV/AIDS.

CHAPTER 18 DREAMS FULFILLED

After the miraculous healing, Bisi got her posting for the National Youth Service Corps' scheme. She was posted to Jigawa state in the northern part of Nigeria. Jigawa state practiced the Islamic sharia law. Her first instinct was to reject the posting. However, because of her new faith in God, she decided to take the offer. She reassured her mother that God would make all things to work together for her good.

Bisi had barely landed on the orientation camp when male Corpers began to throng around her as ants throng sugar. Bisi was indeed looking exceptionally beautiful. There was an aura around her that radiated innocence and love. She naturally attracted both male and female alike. However, because of her harrowing experience with HIV, coupled with her love for God, she made up her mind not to have anything to do with sex until she is married.

"Not anymore! I will not fall into that trap again," she silently vowed.

As the one-month orientation programme gradually came to an end, she had become the talk of the whole camp. The boys couldn't just understand how she could resist and escape their advances. What further got them beaten was that Bisi was such a courteous and respectful lady. In turning down their offers, never once was she rude to any of the boys. This further earned their great respect. Almost spontaneously, the boys nicknamed her 'mama.'

Bisi also drew closer to God in her daily bible study, prayer and attending fellowship. She was elected the vice-president of the Corpers' Christian fellowship.

After the orientation exercise, Bisi was posted to Pneuma Engineering, a reputable engineering firm with branches almost all over the country. Being hardworking, charming and honest, Bisi soon won the heart of her bosses and colleagues.

Propelled with the drive to evolve a science invention before marrying, Bisi gave herself to reading, studying and asking questions from experienced scientists around. She was also a keen observer.

She further cultivated the habit of engaging in personal experimentations. Gradually, she began to acquire some personal laboratory equipment to enable her to continue her experiments at home. With time, she was inspired to embark on a simple DC electric motor project.

"I will make a simple electric motor and thereafter make an electric fan out of it. I will work at it until it is marketable," Bisi echoed as she gazed with determination at the design of the simple electric motor before her.

It was twelve midnight. She stood, pacing to and fro in her single room. She walked to the window and for the umpteenth time looked towards the mountain on the east side of Jigawa city. A cloudy mist was already forming on top of the mountain, with the full moon's reflection sparkling rays of light from the moist mountain top. It was such a beautiful and inspiring sight.

She suddenly felt like worshipping God. Yielding to the urge, she began to sing in a low tone. In her characteristic manner, she was moved to tears in no time. Recalling how God had mercifully delivered her from death, she went on her knees and lifted her hands towards heaven in humble adoration. Bisi had grown to love the Lord over the months. After about thirty minutes of worship, Bisi began to pray. After praying for all her loved ones, she reminded God of her dream, "Father, I pray in Jesus' name, give me understanding, knowledge and wisdom to produce a clever invention that will glorify your name. I desire it Lord, let it happen before I marry. Thank you, Lord for answering my prayer. Amen."

CHAPTER 19 INDIGENOUS FEMALE SCIENCE INVENTOR

One of the objectives of Pneuma Engineering [PEng] was to encourage the active participation of girls in science engineering. PEng management was therefore excited to find the new female corper showing such keen interest in engineering practical work. Not only was Bisi interested in acquiring scientific knowledge, Mr. Pierce, PEng's General Manager, noticed she actually had a drive and creativity to invent. He therefore made it his duty to remind the staff to give Bisi all the necessary support.

With this enabling environment, which Bisi perceived was part of answered prayer, she further committed herself to intense study, experimentation and research within and outside office hours.

Having conceived a topic, she began writing a project plan that incorporated detailed illustrative diagrams. She proceeded with cross-checking her facts from current textbooks in the field of physics and engineering. Thereafter, she commenced practical work after office hours at home.

Bisi still refused to be distracted with sexual relationship. She however had a very intimate female friend called Charity. She was drawn to Charity mainly because of her faith in Christ. Like Bisi, Charity was self-disciplined. Bisi recollected the first time she met Charity at the office restaurant. She was fascinated that Charity had no qualms with openly praying over her food. It was a pleasant surprise finding a pretty young lady with such open display of faith in God. "I'd like to know her better," Bisi decided.

Thereafter, she took her food to her table and greeted her. "Good Afternoon," Bisi chanted with a radiant smile.

"Good Afternoon," Charity responded with an equally radiant smile. Within minutes they were chatting away as if they had known each other for years. That was how their friendship started. The bond was further strengthened when she realized

Charity too was keenly interested in science.

The break periods in the office often found them together and their object of discussion was often their projects. Incidentally their abodes were not far from each other. This, therefore, facilitated deeper interaction.

After close of work, Bisi had a nap. Feeling refreshed after the short rest, Bisi felt a burst of energy. "I should complete this project today. I am almost done."

She pulled out the box containing her mini laboratory gadgets from under her bed and began to set up the simple electric motor unit. "It's this commutator that is giving me a heck of a challenge," she muttered as she fidgeted with one of the copper plate cuttings constituting the commutator. Suddenly, she paused.

Bisi working on her simple electric motor project
"I think I'm missing something somewhere. I remember once

reading about Daniel on how he prayed to God to show him the solution to a problem posed by king Nebuchadnezzar. And God answered his prayer. I think I should pray too."

Bisi knelt down with her elbow on the bed and began to pray. She gave thanks for all that the Lord had been doing in her life and also sang praises unto God. As she was praying and praising God, an idea suddenly crystallized in her mind on how to solve the commutator problem. "Thank you, Jesus," she spontaneously responded as she took her pen to write down the idea. Thereafter she continued worshiping God.

A few hours later, Bisi resumed her project. She felt an excitement in her heart she could not explain. She suddenly had a clear understanding of how to complete the project. Briskly, she screwed the copper plates to the protruding end of the armature. She continued humming praises to God as she soldered the loose ends of the armature coil to the commutator. Next, she bent it into a curvature with the aid of plier. Intermittently she placed the carbon brush fitted perfectly around the curvature of the commutator. Satisfied, she did the same for the second carbon brush. Thereafter, she wound a naked flexible wire smugly around the vertical ends of the carbon brush together with a non-conducting rod that was fitted to the wooden plank on which the simple electric motor model was fixed. The second carbon brush underwent the same treatment. Bisi paused to stretch herself. "The next thing to fix is the rheostat," she decided.

Briskly, Bisi joined one end of the flexible wire coming out of one of the carbon brushes to the positive terminal of the adjustable rechargeable battery she had collected from the office. She picked another strand of flexible wire and joined the negative terminal of the battery to the inlet end of the rheostat. Finally, she joined the flexible wire coming from the second carbon brush to the outlet end of the rheostat to complete the circuit. Meanwhile, the switch controlling the battery was still turned off.

Carefully, Bisi adjusted the power output of the battery to 9 volts. She further checked the whole set-up again, cross-checking with the steps outlined in the physics textbook, open before her.

The magnets had been properly placed, north pole facing south pole across the armature. She ensured the armature was rolling freely around the glass rod that ran through as carriage. The carbon brushes have been firmly fixed such that, as the armature turned, the copper plates were making good contact with them.

Sighing deeply, and stretching back to admire the set-up, Bisi echoed, "The hour has come. It's time for test running." Praying silently under her breath and with her palms breaking out in a cold sweat, she pressed the battery switch to allow electricity to flow through the gadget. Almost instantly, the armature jerked and began to roll gently. It made as if it was going to stop but picked up again. "Eureka! It's working. It's working," Bisi exclaimed and jumped in excitement, oblivious of her environment.

There was a knock on the door, but in her excitement, Bisi did not hear on time. It was Charity's voice that eventually brought her back to reality. "Hold on," she responded as she rushed to the door. Still full of excitement, she flung the door open and swept Charity into her arms.

"What's the excitement about?' Charity wondered as she surveyed the room. Her eyes caught the rolling electric motor on the table. She gasped in disbelief. With equal excitement, she hugged Bisi and they whirled around the room in dancing motion. "Wow! This is marvellous," Charity exclaimed.

"I just started testing it when you arrived. Now let's test the speed," Bisi quipped.

Bending over the set-up, she moved the knob of the rheostat to the left and the speed of the motor reduced drastically. She further moved the motor left until it was hardly moving. Gradually, Bisi moved the knob adjuster to the right and the speed of the motor picked up again until it was rolling very fast. Charity and Bisi screamed with excitement.

"This is simply ingenious," Charity exclaimed. "Congratulations."

"Thank you, Charity. You motivated me you know"

"How?", Charity queried.

"The passion you exhibited for your project and our friendship."

Charity felt elated with her friend's compliment. She was thrilled. She suddenly felt like rushing back to her house to complete her project too. "But no, I have to celebrate with my friend first," she resolved.

"Let's celebrate," Bisi announced as she dipped her head under her bed and pulled out a cartoon. She pulled out a bottle of fruit juice and filled two cups. Raising her cup, she declared a toast. "This is to more ingenious inventions."

Beaming with smile, Charity raised her cup to Bisi's cup. But instead of taking a sip like Bisi has done, Charity gently placed her glass on the stool nearby.

"Bisi, I think we are forgetting something. You know that without the Lord we can do nothing. All good and perfect gifts are from Him. So, I think the first thing we should do is to thank the Lord and give Him all the glory."

With a nudge of guilt, Bisi quickly lowered her glass, nodding in affirmation. "You are definitely right. My! It goes to confirm I am still a babe in the Lord."

"Not to worry. We do forget once in a while," Charity encouraged her.

Charity and Bisi knelt down and lifted up their voices in thanksgiving. They sang praises for some minutes. Bisi eventually rounded up with a prayer of thanksgiving. She also reminded God to help Charity to complete her project too.

It was 9.30 pm before Charity eventually left for her house.

On returning home, Charity made up her mind she would not

sleep until she had made a significant progress on her project. It was as if someone had suddenly injected her with a stimulant. Though she had earlier felt weak from the tiring day's work, a sudden strength was ignited in her. "Oh yes, I must finish the project this week by all means." Charity declared resolutely. So, she set to work.

The following day, Bisi showed her completed project to her boss. The news spread like wildfire. The achievement soon became the talk of the whole establishment. The MD was particularly pleased, seeing the achievement as a vindication of his earlier conviction about Bisi.

CHAPTER 20 SUDDEN CHANGE OF EVENTS

One year after Bisi's breakthrough in making the simple electric motor, she succeeded in perfecting her skill at making electric motors. The motors she made no longer looked unpolished. They were getting closer to the imported motors in appearance. She had also progressed to using the original motor to make table fans. All she did was to replace the spoilt motors in some table fans already declared unserviceable.

Initially she relied on the roadside fan repairers for support. With repeated practice, however, she was able to single-handedly dismantle and reassemble table fans.

While in service, Bisi was able to clear her family's accumulated debts incurred during her HIV/AIDS saga. She was also able to take good care of her mother while helping Tola set up a fishery project. Surprisingly, she was also able to save towards her proposed Master's programme.

This was possible because, apart from the National Youth Service Corp's monthly allowance of ₦7000, Pneuma Engineering further gave her a monthly allowance of ₦20,000. Moreover, Bisi was very prudent in her spending. Unlike most girls of her age, she refused to indulge in excessive dressing. She adopted a simple lifestyle and often denied herself some comforts, all in the bid to achieve her goals.

Tola, Bisi's brother, had begun to harvest and sell fishes of different species to the villagers. Following Bisi's counsel, he began to save in the new Community Bank. It was from the savings he eventually purchased a deep freezer. This enabled him to package the fish in frozen form for sale in the surrounding villages. Abike lived with Tola in the village, but she occasionally visited her daughter Bisi in Jigawa state.

As Bisi was rounding up her youth service, Pneuma Engineering advertised its annual scholarship programme in the National dailies. The scholarship was for a Master's degree in

Engineering fields in Nigerian universities. Notices were posted in university premises all over the country. Trusting God for a miracle, Bisi was amongst the first set of people to submit application for the scholarship programme. In preparation for the screening tests and interview, Bisi began to study, fast and pray.

After a rigorous screening exercise, Bisi was adjudged the most eligible candidate for the scholarship. Five males and five females were selected for the year. Around the same period, Bisi had gained admission to study Electrical Engineering at the University of Lagos. The scholarship covered tuition, books, feeding, accommodation and stipend for some personal needs. Annually, the scholarship was valued at N200,000.

Overjoyed, Bisi felt like travelling to Langbodo to inform her folks about the good news. But it was a Monday. She managed to control her excitement all through the week. 'I will travel this weekend to inform them,' she soliloquized. By 12 noon on Saturday, Bisi was already in Langbodo breaking the good news. Coincidentally, Tola too had just bought a motorcycle to enhance his business. It thus turned out to be a weekend of joy and celebration for the Sokoya family. It was a completely new development for the family, having undergone a catalogue of woes for so many years since the death of their father, Chief Lamidi Sokoya. Recalling how Charity had taught her to show appreciation to God first, Bisi beckoned to Abike and Tola. "The first thing we should do is to give thanks to God for all that He has done for us."

She raised a worship song, "Baba, baba, baba, e se o Baba, e se o baba, a wa dupe Baba." With tears streaming down Bisi's face, she worshipped the Lord. Abike too began to shed tears of joy, recalling all they had suffered.

After they had finished praising and worshipping God, they treated themselves to a sumptuous dinner. Thereafter, Abike and Bisi chatted deep into the night, recalling all the good and bad old times.

"Mama, do you remember the day I lost the money you gave me for Mama Sikira, whilst watching the magician?" They laughed in unison.

"How can I forget? I almost beat you to death, if not for our good neighbours who saved you. But I hope you do understand now why I reacted that way. Times were really hard then."

"Oh yes mama, I do understand now. I shouldn't have been so playful either."

Moving from one episode to another, they chatted on and on. Tola had long gone to bed. The cock had started crowing when they eventually slept. Quite naturally, they woke up late.

Bisi returned to her service station at Berni-Kebbi, Jigawa state on Sunday to enable her to prepare for the new week. She had only a few weeks to round off her National Youth Service Corps' scheme and to commence her Master's degree programme.

Somehow, the news of Bisi's achievement at Pneuma Engineering got to the mass media. Reporters began to pester her for exclusive interviews. Snapshots of her re-enacted efforts at building the simple electric motor and table fan were taken. The interview also covered the scholarship she won.

A few days after, Bisi made headlines in major newspapers in the country. Almost overnight, Bisi became a celebrity. She was the talk of the whole country. At its closing ceremony, the National Youth Service Corps management further honoured her.

By the time she reported for her Master's degree programme, she had become so popular that she hardly needed introduction. Albeit, she was not prepared for the attendant pressures on celebrities. There is the pressure of pride to contend with, as the accolades tend to make a person become 'swollen-headed.' There is also the pressure of trying to meet the unduly high expectations of lecturers and mates who tend to think she is from another planet. And finally, she had to contend with the pressures from the flock of boys who suddenly took interest in striking an intimate relationship with her.

"My focus is clear. I am not going to have an affair until I have completed my formal education. I have not achieved anything yet. I am only just starting," Bisi resolutely reaffirmed.

Without wasting time, she made inquiries about the Christian Fellowships on campus. After praying for guidance, she eventually joined the Central University Christian Fellowship.

Bisi became absorbed in her academics and quest for knowledge of God. She daily prayed to God for understanding, knowledge and wisdom and grew in love for God and fellow man. Bisi continued to be hardworking and self- motivated. She worked beyond the school curriculum. Seeing the challenge, the country was facing concerning electricity, she gradually developed interest in the generation of alternative energy. She was encouraged by Pneuma Engineering to make use of its facility anytime she needed to. Bisi occasionally travelled to the company's branch office in Ibadan to make up for some lacking practical equipment in her department. So, she commenced the building of a dynamo.

She came out best in all her courses at the end of the first semester examination.

One of her hostel mates, Comfort, who had been watching her closely with keen interest, asked her one day, "Bisi, tell me, how are you able to manage it? I mean you a female being able to excel so well in engineering?"

Smiling, Bisi answered, "It is simple, I daily ask God for help. I trust Him for answers, and then I give myself to hard work in my study and practical works."

Comfort shook her head in disbelief. "It sounds too easy to be true."

Bisi encouraged her, "You try it. It has worked for me these few years I have known Him. I know it will work for you too."

Bisi continued with her inventions. By the time she was rounding up her Masters' programme, she had three useful marketable products to her credit – a simple electric motor/a fan, an electricity generating dynamo and solar-powered electric generator.

The speed of events and activities made one year look like a fleeting moment. Bisi could hardly believe she had completed the programme all too soon.

It was already time for the graduation ceremony. Bisi invited Abike, Tola and a number of relatives for the ceremony. The Pneuma Engineering was duly represented too. Even the MD was present. The reporters thronged her. Everyone wanted a word with her. Bisi collected the special award for the best female student in Engineering.

A few weeks before rounding off her Masters' programme,

Bisi was nominated as one of the Consultants to the United Nations Girls' Science Education programme. A week after graduation, Bisi was on board Nigeria Airways heading for UNESCO Headquarters in Paris to commence her consultancy assignment. It was her first flight ever.

She was still struggling with her seat belt, when she suddenly noticed a copper coloured strong arm stretching across her lap to assist her in hooking the seat belt.

With a gentle baritone voice, the young man whispered, "Can I help you?" The fragrance of a sweet-smelling perfume wafted across her nose. She pulled herself back to give room for the man. In the process, she had a good look at the person helping her.

For the first time since her experience with Tunde, Bisi felt her heartbeat skip. She knew the reaction too well. Without making a pass at her, this young handsome man had touched a soft spot in her being. Almost involuntarily, Bisi found herself wishing he would strike a conversation with her. The opportunity came when she had to grip the arm of her chair when the plane was about to take off. Unconsciously she clasped the young man's hand with the armrest. Turning sideways with an understanding smile, the young man remarked,

"I guess this is your first flight."

With a trembling voice Bisi answered, "You are right."

"Don't worry, you will soon get used to it. Just relax."

When the plane had taken off and stabilized, Bisi relaxed. After the breakfast had been served, Bisi's travelling companion cleared his throat and said, "My name is Bayo. Bayo Omotosho. What about you?"

"I am Bisi, Bisi Sokoya."

That was how Bisi and Bayo began to chat. They hardly ceased conversation all through the flight.

In the course of their discussion they discovered they had so many things in common. They were both in the field of Electrical Engineering, hailed from the same state, born in the same month of July, though Bayo was five years earlier.

They were both born-again Christians.

Bayo had a doctorate degree in Electrical and Electronic Engineering. He was a lecturer at the Ahmadu Bello University, Zaria, Nigeria. The interesting part of it all was that Bayo was on his way to Paris to report for a Consultancy appointment too.

Presently, the plane had begun to descend. They quickly scribbled their addresses in Paris. They almost collapsed in laughter when they realized they had written the same address.

"It seems fate has brought us together for a purpose," Bayo remarked.

Bisi felt her heartbeat skipping again. 'O God, what is happening to me?' She thought. Deliberately, she allowed the remark to pass without a comment but rather looked away to prevent him from detecting her feeling.

The Pilot's voice suddenly came on the loudspeakers. "Attention please. We are 2,000 feet above sea level. We are about to land in one of the most beautiful cities in the world. Some call it, lovers' city."

Almost impulsively Bayo and Bisi exchanged looks. It was as if the Pilot was confirming their thoughts. Bayo smiled, exposing beautifully set teeth. Blushing, Bisi quickly looked away.

The Pilot continued, "Ladies and gentlemen, please fasten your seatbelts as we shall landing in the next five minutes."

Bisi found the meeting with Bayo mysterious, almost strange. For the past three years, she had succeeded in controlling her feelings and emotions, even whilst on campus where the temptations were so strong. "Why then am I suddenly feeling so incapable of controlling myself with Bayo? Why, why, why? Lord I need an explanation," she silently prayed as the plane landed.

The landing was so smooth that even Bisi, a first timer with flight, was not aware the plane had landed. It was only when she heard the swooshing sound of the windbreakers and the screeching tyres that she became conscious of what was happening. Out of fear, she impulsively gripped Bayo's right hand that was resting on the armrest.

Gently patting her hand, Bayo re-assured her, "Relax Bisi. Don't be afraid. The bird is already on the ground and is trying to taxi to a final stop."

His confident yet gentle voice instantly allayed her fears. She gently pulled away her hand from under his. At that instant, a strange thought seemed to form in her mind. It was strange because it was as if someone was speaking to her. "Bayo is your husband," the voice seemed to say. Unconsciously, she reacted aloud, "No way."

Bayo was curious, "No way to what?"

Embarrassed, she quickly thought of a cover up, "Oh, it's nothing. I was just thinking aloud."

By this time, passengers had started alighting. Not long after, they were in the arrival lounge and almost instantly they spotted their names boldly written on placards. Within minutes, they were in the hotel.

Just before parting ways, Bayo walked up to Bisi and shook her hand, "Bisi, I am really happy to meet you. See you at dinner, okay?"

Almost in a murmur, she responded, "Okay."

The moment she entered her room and locked the door she dropped to her knees in prayer. "Lord. I need your help. That thought coming to mind about Bayo being my husband. I want a confirmation from you Lord. Is it the imagination of my heart or it is your Spirit speaking to my heart? Dear Lord, please let me know. You know I cannot afford to make another mistake. Please Lord answer me"

Hardly realizing how tired she was, coupled with jetlag, she did not realize when she dozed off whilst on her knees. Thereafter, she found herself walking down the aisle of a large church in a wedding gown. By her side, in navy blue suit, was

Bayo. There was a large crowd of witnesses. Everyone was joyous. They were about to kiss in response to the Pastor's instruction that they should seal the marriage with a kiss, when the telephone bell woke her.

She could hardly believe she had been dreaming. It was so real. Recalling her prayer before dozing, she instantly concluded that it was the answer to her prayers. As she walked towards the phone, she reassured herself, "I will not rush through it though. I must confirm the will of God in other ways. I simply can't afford to make another silly mistake."

On entering his room, Bayo knelt down and gave thanks to God for a safe journey to Paris and for the meeting with Bisi. Somehow, he perceived it was not a casual meeting. With over ten years of walking with the Lord, he knew when the Lord was leading him into something. Of course, he had been praying for some months now on the issue of finding a life partner. He began to unpack whilst thinking about Bisi.

"She is truly a unique lady. There is something about her that seems to naturally attract me. If what I perceive is correct, I think I have finally met my wife. But I must pray and confirm this. With three nasty mistakes behind me, I just can't afford to make another mistake."

"There is no time to waste," he decided. He stopped unpacking and began to worship God. After some minutes, he went down on his knees and began to pray. "Oh, Lord God, I appreciate all you have been doing in my life. I appreciate the way you have been guiding me, your favour brought me to Paris, at this time. I know there is no accident with you. You ordered our steps into your divine will and purpose each time. I do not want to be presumptuous, particularly over this issue. I have been praying to you on this matter for some months now and I know you have heard my prayers. Father, I ask in the name of my Lord Jesus that you grant me confirmation of my perception. Have I met my wife at last? Is Bisi the lady you have chosen to be my helpmeet?"

He kept quiet before the Lord for some time, and suddenly felt a spring of joy and peace in his heart that seemed to go beyond the natural. He knew from experience that he had got the witness of the Spirit on this issue. He prostrated on the rug before the Lord and began to thank God for the answered prayer.

"Yet, for all these, I am not going to take chances. Not with the kind of mistakes I made in the past. I will yet seek other ways to confirm this is truly from the Lord," Bayo resolutely made up his mind as he stood up to get ready for dinner. "I won't rush this!"

With this resolution, he proceeded to unpack his belongings. Thereafter he shaved and dived into the showers. With the consciousness that he would soon be joining Bisi for dinner, he carefully chose his apparel and cologne. Whistling under his breath, he began to dress. Making a final check in the mirror to ensure everything was properly placed, he walked up to the telephone set and dialed the operator requesting to be linked with Bisi's room.

CHAPTER 23 PARADOX

It was five years since Bisi met Bayo on the way to Paris. They had since returned to Nigeria, married and had two children, but not until they confirmed it was God's will and passed the HIV test. Bisi insisted on the latter despite Bayo's efforts at convincing her otherwise. His reasoning was that once the Lord had confirmed they were meant for one another, every other thing must be right about the relationship.

Bisi recalled the events of the past five years with a smile. Like a whirlwind, their love had soared higher and higher until they could no longer hide it. Eventually, Bayo proposed. Before the end of the consultancy programme, they were officially engaged. They had begun to prepare for the wedding whilst the consultancy programme was rounding off. Most of the wedding materials were purchased in Paris.

The wedding had taken place a month after returning to Nigeria. It was grand and colourful. It was a celebrities wedding. The mass media covered the event.

Presently, Bisi stretched back and for the umpteenth time, looked at the wedding picture that hung over her office wall. As usual, her gaze dwelled on Bayo. She had grown so fond of him over the years. Reflecting, she mused, 'I don't know what I would do without Bayo. Lord, I thank you for giving me such a wonderful husband. I can't ask for a better one. Truly, it has been heaven on earth for us. It's the Lord's doing, and it is marvelous in my eyes.'

The phone rang, Bisi picked up the receiver, "Hello, this is Biba Engineering."

"Can I speak with Engr. (Mrs.) Bisi Omotosho?"

"Speaking…"

"I am Chief Farakan, Oba Obembe, the king of Langbodo sent me to you. I would like to see you to deliver the king's message.

It can't be discussed on the phone."

Bisi was pensive. "What could it be about," she thought. "Uhmmm … sir, I will discuss with my husband and get back to you. What is your phone number?"

"333222. I will await your call," the Chief replied and hung up.

With excitement Bisi lifted the intercom's receiver and dialed Bayo's number. With the proceeds of their consultancy jobs and the royalties on their successful products, they had set up an engineering firm in Lagos after their wedding. They have been doing well ever since. Bisi had more control over her time. She could take care of Bayo and her children and yet have ample time for her research and campaign against the spread of HIV/AIDS.

"Hello," Bayo's baritone voice came on the line. "Hello darling. I just got a strange call from one Chief Farakan. He said he is representing Oba Obembe, the king of Langbodo. He desired a formal meeting to deliver a special message from the king. I felt I should discuss it with you first."

"Darling, thanks for honouring me. What do you think? Shouldn't we hear what it's all about?"

"I think we should. But at what time and place?" Bisi quipped.

"Invite him to your office, during break tomorrow," Bayo replied.

"That sounds okay with me. I will get back to the Chief then," Bisi paused then added, "Bayo, I love you."

"I love you too Bisi, very much," Bayo replied and hung up.

Bisi got back to Chief Farakan and fixed the appointment. By twelve noon the following day, Chief Farakan and three other persons [a male and two females] had arrived at Biba Engineering.

When they were all comfortably seated and served with soft drinks, Bayo opened the discussion. "I am Bayo Omotosho and here is my wife, Engr. (Mrs.) Bisi Omotosho. May we know your mission sir?"

Chief Farakan stood up smiling. He cleared his throat and began to introduce his entourage. "Meet Chief (Mrs.) Odenla, Chief Bebeniyi and Chief (Mrs.) Ofon. Our mission is simple. Oba Obembe, the paramount king of Langbodo, has decided to honour your wife with a chieftaincy title, the Iya Asiwaju of Langbodo."

He dipped his hand into his overall's pocket and brought out a sealed letter which he handed over to Bisi.

Bisi stood up, collected it, curtseying. She then passed the letter to her husband. Bayo collected the letter feeling honoured. His respect for Bisi soared. He opened the letter and drew close to Bisi, such that they could read the content together. It was the same message delivered by the Chief with embellishments on the good works Bisi has done over the years. The king personally signed the letter.

Responding, Bayo said, "We feel highly honoured by the kind gesture of the king. We however crave your indulgence to think about the offer. We shall personally visit the king with our reply?"

"That is ok with us. We shall await your response," Chief Farakan replied as he and his entourage stood up to leave.

When they had gone, Bayo asked, "Bisi, what do you think?"

"Whatever you say darling. I find the whole issue quite interesting. To think that it is from the same village where I had been ridiculed, mocked and treated like an outcast that I am now found worthy of honour. Nevertheless, I strongly feel our faith contradicts their traditional chieftaincy practices. We can hardly serve God and 'mammon,' can we?" Bisi replied.

"That is exactly what was going on in my mind. But the question is how do we express our views to the king without offending him and his Chiefs?"

After thinking a while, Bisi said, "Let us politely tell the king that we appreciate his kind gesture and would be ready to assist the village in any way we can, but as ministers of God, we may not be able to accept the chieftaincy. We can back it up with fasting and prayer for favour."

"That sounds plausible to me," Bayo agreed.

Thus, Bisi and Bayo rescinded the chieftaincy offer. She focused on her faith, family and her career. She further intensified her campaign against the spread of HIV/AIDS.

Working harmoniously with her husband, Biba Engineering evolved many more scientific inventions. They gave their children an early start in the same field.

Bisi and Bayo were happy and fulfilled.

Bisi, Bayo and their four children – two boys and two girls

TODAY

Today is the most important day of your life Yesterday is gone, gone forever

Tomorrow is hardly real for when it comes it changes its name to TODAY

The future you are awaiting is TODAY. TODAY, therefore is your only reality

The way you use TODAY therefore determines your destiny

Without controversy, TODAY IS THE MOST IMPORTANT DAY OF YOUR LIFE

Learn to make the best of TODAY by making every moment count.

Source:
Dr. Dayo Odukoya
dayoodukoya@gmail.com
+2349096505735 (Whatsapp)